SOLOMON'S KITTEN

Moments after she is born, tiny kitten Tallulah, with her bright eyes and silver and white fur edged with gold, is whisked away from her father Solomon and dumped in the hedge like rubbish. After a tough start to life, neglected and abandoned, Tallulah eventually finds a new home with the Lee family and forms a special bond with their daughter Tammy. But Tammy has a terrible secret and Tallulah must do all in her power to keep the family safe.

SOLOMON'S KITTEN

SOLOMON'S KITTEN

by

Sheila Jeffries

Magna Large Print Books
Long Preston, North Yorkshire,
BD23 4ND, England.

British Library Cataloguing in Publication Data.

Jeffries, Sheila
    Solomon's kitten.

    A catalogue record of this book is
    available from the British Library

    ISBN   978-0-7505-4152-7

First published in Great Britain by
Simon & Schuster UK Ltd., 2014

Published in Large Print 2015 by arrangement with
Simon & Schuster UK Ltd.

Magna Large Print is an imprint of Library Magna Books Ltd.

Printed and bound in Great Britain by
T.J. (International) Ltd., Cornwall, PL28 8RW

*To my amazing husband, Ted,
my soulmate and friend*

It was a girl kitten, fluffy and very beautiful, with tinges of silver and gold in her fur.

'This is a special kitten,' said my angel. 'She's come here to heal, like you, Solomon.' So, in those moments before Jessica came back for her, I gave the tabby kitten lots of love and purring. One day she opened her baby-blue eyes and looked at me as if she wanted to fix me in her memory for ever.

It was the last happy day I remember. The house felt sunlit and peaceful. Ellen and Joe were friends, and John was playing happily in the garden.

And that was the day the bailiff came.

Extract from *Solomon's Tale*

Chapter One

'FOLLOW THAT GIRL'

'Follow that girl,' said my angel.

The girl was crying as she hurried past me. She was staring at the ground in front of her, and clutching a white plastic bag with something heavy inside. Whatever it was, I could smell it, and it was alive. Every time she met someone, she tightened her grip on the bag and twisted past them. She seemed afraid of being stopped.

I was sitting on the garden wall under an orange street light, a good place for a cat to watch the life of the street, and catch the moths that flitted around the honeysuckle. I was a young cat, a bit nervous as I'd had a bad start to my life, and I rarely ventured outside our square of garden.

My angel's voice buzzed through my whiskers and made my silver and white fur bush out with courage. I jumped down from the wall and ran after the crying girl. Instinct told me to do it furtively, so I crept on quiet paws through front gardens, under gates and hedges, over fences and under parked cars. I stalked the girl by listening to the tip-tap of her shoes, the sniff-sniff of her crying, and the strange animal smell that came from the big bag. It was the subtle smell of fear that told me this was important.

My silver tabby fur made perfect camouflage in the summer twilight. Only my white bits and socks gave me away. The traffic frightened me, but I kept following the girl through a maze of streets. Would I ever find my way home?

She turned into an alleyway, and paused under a lamp. She lit a fag and I could see her hands shaking as the smoke curled upwards in the orange light. She had put the bag down. I peeped round the gatepost where I was hiding. I stared at the bag on the floor.

And then it moved.

Something inside kicked and wriggled, rustling the plastic. That really spooked me. With my soft fur brushing the ground, I crept nearer. Grizzly little cries of distress were coming from inside the bag. Some kind of creature in there was lonely and desperate.

The girl responded by snatching up the bag and marching on with it.

'Shut up,' she hissed. 'Just SHUT UP, will

you?' Even in the dark, her aura looked like cracked glass.

I dashed after her down a long footpath to where the streetlights ended and a white moon shone over the common, glinting on hummocks of rough grass and bramble leaves. I could smell the dogs who were walked there, and it sharpened my awareness. Scared now, I hid in the long grass and watched the girl's shadow. There was danger. A tang of water, a sound that rushed and babbled through the night, a sense of mysterious river creatures who lived there and emerged when it was dark. I could see the glimmer of water, and the arch of a high bridge. Horrified, I watched the girl walk over it, and stop right in the middle. She opened the plastic bag.

I knew what she was going to do, and I remembered how it felt to a living creature to be tipped out like rubbish. I ran closer, and sat majestically on the path, staring at her, using my cat power and meowing.

The girl turned and saw me. Then her crying started again in loud sobs.

'I can't do this,' she howled, and came down from the bridge, hunched over with the crying, the bag clutched against her body. Nearby was an elder tree growing out of a wall, and she disappeared under the shadow of its branches.

Minutes later, she emerged without the bag, her arms wrapped around herself as if every bone in her body was hurting.

'Fluff your fur,' said my angel, 'put your tail up and run to meet her.'

So I did. It wasn't difficult. I knew how appealing I would look, a silver and white cat with long fur and golden eyes that shone in the moonlight. Like a spirit cat.

We met on the path and I gazed up at her and meowed in a friendly way. She froze. Then she reached down and stroked me. I patted the gold and silver bangles that jangled round her wrist. I sniffed her finger, and it had that smell on it, the salty tang of something newly born.

'Hello,' she whispered. 'Magic puss cat.'

I liked that name. Better than 'Fuzzball', which is what my human had called me. I mean – Fuzzball? – for me, the Queen of Cats! And I liked the way the girl looked so deeply into my eyes. I looked into hers, and what I saw was pure beauty ensnared in suffering, like a lacewing caught in a spider's web.

'Remember her,' said my angel softly. 'One day, you will need to find her again.'

So I kept staring, fixing the essence of her soul into mine. No matter how much she changed her hair and clothes, I would still know her by the blend of pain and magic in her eyes.

'Don't follow me,' she said, moving on restlessly, her heartbeat loud, her tears glinting in the moonlight. I jumped onto the wall and ran along beside her with my tail up. I meowed until she stopped again and turned her face up to me. We touched noses. I had bonded with her.

'Don't follow me, magic puss cat,' she said again. 'If you knew what I'd done, you wouldn't want to know me. Don't follow me, I'm BAD NEWS. Evil. That's what I am.'

I purred and purred, pouring my love into her and my purring was a stream of healing stars. Weaving to and fro, I rubbed my whole body against her crying face until she smiled just a little and told me her name.

'TammyLee.'

Fascinated, I listened to the rhythm of the name. I patted the gold bead in the side of her nose, and played with a wisp of her hair. TammyLee. I didn't care what evil she had done. In that moment, my job was to love.

We ran on together through the night, me on the wall and she on the path, and we were wishing I could be her cat. But when we reached the orange streetlights again, a change came over TammyLee. She stopped crying, lifted her head, and began marching along with her shoes clonking. Her aura hardened to a shell and I noticed a man walking rapidly towards her.

'Where the hell have you been, Tammy-Lee?' he asked.

She shrugged.

'Nowhere, Dad. Don't FUSS.'

'We've been worried sick. You've got school in the morning, my girl.'

'Who cares?'

'We do. You rushed out of the house complaining of stomach pains, then you disappear for FOUR hours. Why was your mobile switched off? Your mum is getting herself in such a state worrying about you, and it doesn't help her illness, does it? And I don't need to be out here combing the streets all hours of the night, TammyLee. You're only fourteen, for goodness' sake.'

'I'm fourteen and I need a LIFE,' Tammy-Lee shouted.

'Don't you get bolshy with me, my girl.'

'I'm not being bolshy, Dad. I'm upset.'

'What about?'

'STUFF.'

'What stuff?'

'Stuff you don't understand.' TammyLee turned and marched off, her face set like a doll. 'OK, OK, I'm going home.'

I hesitated. I wanted to follow, but instead I watched the man walk after her, muttering something about teenagers. He looked bewildered and he didn't give me a passing glance.

I sat on the wall, thinking, as I watched them go down the street. I was a lucky cat. I had a decent home with an old lady, even if she did call me Fuzzball. She fed me and fussed over me, I was safe there, and I was free. Right now, I loved being out in the moonlight, so, yes, I was going to see what was in that bag. I could feel it drawing me, calling to me.

Wild creatures lived on the common; foxes, rats, stoats and weasels. And crows. Something in that bag was alive, and I had to get to it before they did. With my tail looped and my ears flat, I bolted back across the common, and when I came close to the elder tree growing out of the wall, I was spooked and flattened myself against the ground.

The bag gleamed white against the tree trunk. It was wide open. I stalked it on quiet paws, my whiskers twitching, my fur stiff with nervousness. I peeped in, and drew back, shocked.

A baby. A human baby was in there. Very tiny, red-faced, with its little fists waving. It was cold, and hungry. What could I do?

I eased myself into the bag and covered the baby's body with my warm fur and my purring. I would keep him warm, show him that someone cared. I would stay there until morning, until someone came.

I settled down to wait until dawn, my warm body spread out like a rug over the tiny baby, and I could feel his warmth under me, the rapid pulsing of his heart. Carefully leaving a space for him to breathe, I shut my eyes and purred, glad to be helping this new little being. For I knew only too well how it felt to be abandoned.

Before I came to this planet, I lived in the spirit world, and I was a shining cat.

Shining cats are the souls of real cats, living in the spirit world between lifetimes. Some call the spirit world heaven, and in a way it is. It's peaceful and warm, full of colours and music, and we don't have to worry about physical bodies. There's no illness or hunger, no fleas or trips to the vet, and no arguments. We communicate by telepathy, which is easy and quick. And we get to work with the angels and that gives us a real buzz.

In the spirit world I still looked like a cat, but I was very light, like thistledown, and my face was surrounded by a halo of gold and silver, like fur, but made of light. I was a very important cat. I sat majestically on a violet cushion, and all the shining cats in the spirit world would gather around me for communal purring sessions that sent ripples across the universe.

I was the Queen of Cats.

I only agreed to be born again on earth because no other cat would go. The task was to experience abandonment, and then to help reunite an abandoned child with its mother. It sounded impossible, which is why I thought I could do it. No problem. And I had an angel, a new one who introduced herself as the Angel of Secrets.

She was clear as glass and her robe rustled with stars of turquoise, emerald and lime. Camouflage, she said, to blend with the colours of earth's oceans and forests.

'When you are on earth, I will always be with you,' she said in a voice that tinkled like bells. 'But my colours and my transparency will help me to hide, and you must remember that and work hard to see me. My voice will blend with the sound of rain, and the wind in the leaves, so you must listen for me, and not get distracted by the cacophony of noise that humans manage to create.'

When it was time for me to be born as an earth kitten, I was nervous about whizzing through the star gates, having to let go and burst through the golden web. I didn't feel I could do it. So my angel led me through a beautiful land where shining cats and dogs were playing and resting, and eventually, we arrived at the foot of the rainbow bridge, which was awesome.

'Choose a colour,' she said, 'and you can just walk over with your tail up.'

I hesitated, staring up at the arched bridge of glowing colours. I sat and watched it for a while, reassured to see other cats, and dogs, trotting over confidently, some going, some arriving. All of them were quiet and peaceful.

'Once you start, you can't go back,' my angel explained, 'so take your time, and all will be well. Trust me, I'm an angel.'

Still I hesitated, and she said, 'Why not choose pink? It's the colour of love. You can't go wrong with that.'

I put one shining paw into the pink light, and before I knew it, I was walking, tail up, higher and higher over the rainbow bridge.

Easy! Over the top, and there in the distance, far below me was Planet Earth. I wanted to cry because she looked utterly delicate and complex, her colours magical. Electric blues, rich greens, lemon and lots of white.

But as I reached the summit, my angel swirled past me with a whoosh of her wings. Shocked, I watched her disappear, her colours shimmering as she dissolved and became one with the landscapes of Planet Earth. I couldn't stop now. I was racing, sliding down the other side of the rainbow bridge; it took my breath away; even though I knew how it would happen, I was still terrified.

I didn't want my fabulous spirit to be put inside a tiny wriggling earth kitten. I wanted to go back and be the Queen of Cats for ever. But it was too late. Being born was such a let-down. I should have been loved – and I wasn't!

I was born under someone's bed, right next to a smelly pair of slippers. And my mother didn't like me. The minute I was born, she gave me a draconian swipe with her paw, knocking my small wet head sideways. I was blind, but I sensed her anger as I struggled to breathe. She was blaming me for getting stuck and causing her pain. Weak and shocked, I lay there on my own, getting colder and colder.

A man's voice made me jump.

'Ellen!' he was shouting. 'Guess what THAT CAT'S DONE NOW!'

'What?'

'She's had a bunch of kittens under the bed.'

'Oh, Jessica!'

Ellen's voice was lovely. I heard her come and look under the bed. 'Oh, the little darlings,' she whispered. 'Don't be cross with her, Joe. We can take them downstairs in a basket. Aw, look at them feeding. Aren't you a clever girl, Jessica?'

I was cold and starving so I squeaked and squeaked until Ellen noticed me, and I felt her hand round me.

'What about this one, Jessica?' She put me down close to my two purring guzzling brothers, and gently pushed my face into my mother's fur. 'No, don't growl at her, Jessica. She's beautiful. Silver tabby with long fur and she's got pink paws like you. Come on, you've got to feed her.'

I found a nipple and sucked like mad until the warm sweet milk filled my mouth and mother finally relaxed and let me have it while Ellen stayed close, encouraging her. I got the feeling that Jessica was rebellious but she would do anything for Ellen. So I was fed. But Jessica never liked me. She always left me until last, lavishing attention on my two brothers, and she would bop me when Ellen wasn't there. Twice we were put in a nice basket and carried downstairs, and both times Jessica carried us back, one by one, holding us by the scruff. When it was my turn, she wasn't careful. She banged me all up the stairs.

On that day, before our eyes were open, there was a lot of shouting and crying in the house, and we all lay there shivering, cuddling close and wondering what was going to happen. What kind of home had we come into so trustingly?

At the end of the day, I heard this amazing loud purring, and sensed a huge male cat very close, looking at us, sniffing us. He was loving and kind, I knew that, but my mother still growled at him until he backed off. Once our eyes were open, I saw him. He was black with a white chest and paws, long white whiskers and concerned pea-green eyes. His aura was massive and shining. My dad! Solomon.

I settled down, thinking I had decent parents and a warm safe home, even if there was a lot of shouting. The three of us grew up under the bed, learning to crawl, to put our tails up and to play. We got used to Ellen and her little boy, John, picking us up. In fact, we loved it. They were so warm and kind and stroked our fur and talked to us.

Until one terrible day that I will never forget.

We were four weeks old and just learning to lap Kitty Milk from a dish. Jessica was a strict mother. She bopped us if we put our feet in it, and she diligently kept us immaculate, always leaving me until last. Sometimes our dad Solomon would come and wash me, and purr with me and tell me stuff by telepathy.

On that day, the house shook like thunder, and two strange men plodded in and out, moving furniture, sliding and scraping and bumping it down the stairs. Then Joe came in with a basket in his hand. He put it down on the bedroom floor and reached under the bed where we were cuddled together against our mother's warm body.

'Sorry about this, Jessica,' he said, and picked us up one by one with his big hand and dumped us inside the basket. I saw my mother's anxious eyes as she came after us, and that was the last time I ever saw her dear black and white face. She cried and cried as Joe clipped the basket shut. He slammed the bedroom door and we heard Jessica's echoing wail of despair, and her paws scrabbling to get out.

We huddled together and clung on with our tiny paws as he bounded down the stairs swinging the basket.

'There's nothing to cry about,' he said to Ellen and John, 'so stop your snivelling. We've got more to worry about than a bunch of kittens.'

He took us outside, and that was the first time I saw the sky and smelled the lawn. A bird was singing high up in one of the trees, and women and children were walking past with pushchairs. No one seemed to care about us, three kittens suddenly wrenched away from their mother. Jessica was at the window, crying and crying, clawing at the glass with her pink paws.

'You will take them to the Cat Sanctuary, won't you?' said Ellen to Joe.

'Course I will. Stop fussing.' Joe swung the basket into a car and another door was banged in our faces. Seriously worried now, we were climbing all over the inside of the basket, desperately seeking a crack or a hole through which we could escape.

The inside of the car smelled of beer and socks. It squealed and rattled as Joe drove us away from our home and our mother, away from Solomon, away from Ellen and John. We travelled fast, the basket lurching as the car hurtled round corners. We grew hot with fear and exhausted by our efforts to escape.

'Nearly there, guys,' said Joe. He hauled the car around a sharp bend and slowed down. 'Here we are. Cat Sanctuary.'

He turned the engine off, and there was only the sound of our three baby voices crying and crying for our mother cat. Joe swung the basket out of the car and walked towards a pair of high wire gates. He stopped in front of them, looking at a notice board.

And then he exploded.

'SHIT,' he bellowed. 'They're shitting CLOSED.'

He kicked at the wire gates. He put the basket down and rattled the gates with both hands.

'What's the good of a cat sanctuary that's CLOSED!' he roared. 'Well, you'll have to go somewhere. I've gotta get back. I can't be doing with a bunch of wailing cats.'

He flung our basket into the hedge. Then he got back into the car, reversed it and roared off, filling the lane with black smoke and a storm of gravel.

And he left us there, three terrified kittens

cowering in a corner of the basket.

Minutes later, the car came racing back and skidded to a halt. Joe got out, swigging beer from a can. Still swearing, he seized our basket, opened it and tipped us out like rubbish into the long wet grass.

Chapter Two

A BAD CAT

I learned a lot during those lonely hours in the hedge.

My brothers were both black; they were mates and didn't care about me, so I followed them as they crawled deep into the hedge. We had to keep each other warm. We found a dry twiggy hollow at the roots of a hawthorn tree and pressed close together. Hungry and tired, we slept, and when we woke, nothing had changed except the sunlight, which was now a brassy pink. We'd grown up under a bed, and we hadn't learned about day and night, earth and sky, sun and rain.

Soon we were starving. We spent the night creeping about, not far away from each other, tasting anything we could find; worms, slugs, beetles, all disgusting and too tough for our delicate new teeth. We licked raindrops from the leaves and blades of grass, and we did a lot of meowing, hoping our mother would come and find us.

I tried to see my angel, but I was too little to remember how. Her voice whispered to me, but it wasn't anything I wanted to hear.

'Your mother is far away,' she said. 'Jessica and Solomon were put in the basket and taken away, hundreds of miles. You won't see them again in this lifetime.'

But she coaxed me out in the morning to feel the sun on my fur, and this time my brothers followed me. We sat at the edge of the lane on hot stones, and the sun's warmth was a new and healing experience for us. The sound of a dog barking sent us scurrying back to our twiggy hollow. I'd never seen a real dog and, curious, I crawled out on my own through the narrow grass tunnel we'd made.

I peeped, and immediately regretted it. Towering over me was a very stiff black Labrador with such a tail, wagging up in the sky. Its ears were up and its brown eyes were staring at me. It gave a soft huffy sort of woof and its hot breath gusted over me. Too petrified to move, I stared back and we had a telepathic exchange. She was an old dog, wise and kindly; she wanted to tell me something, and she wanted to ask me a question. Her eyes were puzzled, as if she knew I shouldn't be there.

'Come on, Harriet. Whatever it is, leave it. I said LEAVE IT,' called a voice from further down the lane.

Harriet gave an apologetic shrug, turned and trotted off, looking back at me just once, her paw in the air.

'LEAVE IT,' shouted the voice again. I was trembling with shock at my first encounter with a dog. The overwhelming smell of her, the thickness of her legs, the way she went stiff when she saw me. And yet, tiny as I was, I had a sudden sense of power. I was a CAT. Well, almost.

Two more days and nights passed. We kept each other warm, but we were getting weaker and more depressed. We'd given up meowing; it took too much energy. Worse than that was the emotional pain. That feeling of being dumped in the hedge like rubbish never left me in my whole life, but weaved and wandered through my aura in strands of anger and sorrow. We should have been normal happy little cats, but already, at four weeks old, our confidence was damaged, our sense of self-worth shaken. And we didn't have our mother to teach us how to live.

I wondered if Jessica ever got over losing us, even me.

On our third day in the hedge, something terrifying happened.

We were sleeping, heaped together in a mound of fur, in a round nest we had made in the grass, when I woke up suddenly. The Labrador, Harriet, was looming over us, puffing and sniffing, a long pink tongue flopping from her mouth. I caught the smell and the gleam of her teeth set in pink and black shiny gums, and the look of thoughtfulness in her eyes as she reached down to me. Before I could move, she had opened her jaws and picked me up by the scruff.

I squealed and screeched. My heart lurched into a stream of beats. I tried to kick and scratch but she had me so tightly, stretching my skin so that my tiny legs splayed out and wouldn't move. I hung there, hardly able to breathe, and the dog lifted me high in the air and walked off with me.

'I can't survive this. I can't,' I thought, panicking. But Harriet was plodding down the lane with me. She wasn't going to put me down. I kept my baby-blue eyes wide open, and floating alongside us were splinters of coloured light, stars of turquoise, emerald and lime. My angel! My angel was there, escorting us in cloaks of light, and in total silence. The Angel of Secrets.

After that, I calmed down and let it happen. Harriet wasn't eating me. She was taking me somewhere, the only way she knew how, in her mouth. An extraordinary thought dawned in me: this was a dog, a dear old dog who wanted to mother me.

She broke into a trot, and I was swinging, like it was when Jessica had carried me upstairs. I could see the dog's tail wagging faster and faster. We reached a wicket gate in the hedge, and Harriet shoved it open with her paw, being careful not to bump me. She took me up a garden path and in through an open door.

'Oh, Harriet! What have you got?'

A woman was sitting there on a cosy sofa. Harriet's tail dropped and only the tip of it wagged apologetically as she gently put me down in the woman's lap. I lay there in total shock. The woman's lap smelled of bread and flowers. She gasped.

'A KITTEN!'

I sat there, disorientated.

'Where did you get that from?' she asked

Harriet loudly. And immediately the dog turned around and bounded out, her tail wagging madly. She turned the corner on one leg and galloped up the lane.

'What a little beauty you are,' whispered the woman. She cupped me gently in a pair of weathered hands, and I could have cried. The way she looked at me with such tenderness. Someone wanted me. I wasn't rubbish. The dog hadn't hurt me.

Minutes later, Harriet came back through the door, her tail bang banging against the wood, and in her mouth was one of my brothers. She did the same again. Put the traumatised kitten down next to me and charged out again to fetch the other one.

'That dog!' Tears were running down the woman's face. 'That dog is a miracle. A miracle.'

But this time the dog returned with a puzzled expression on her face, and she hadn't got my brother. He was the all-black one, the biggest and bravest of us three kittens.

I never saw him again.

I'd have liked to stay in the cottage and cuddled up to Harriet for the rest of my life, but it wasn't to be. A few days later, well fed and rested, we were put in another basket and taken, gently this time, to a Cat Rescue Centre, to await adoption.

I wanted to go with my brother. He was all I had. But the first person to look at us fell in love with me straight away. Her name was Gretel. I gazed up at her wrinkled face which was covered in powder, and her expectant eyes under blue-painted lids. Two tantalising pearls dangled from her ears and there was a halo of silvery hair. She pursed her red-painted lips, then opened her mouth very wide.

'Oh, what a pretty kitten. Aren't you a little poppet?' she crooned, and picked me up as if I was made of gold. She held me against her pale pink sweater, and I managed to keep still, smelling her perfume and watching those earrings. Aware that my silver and white fur was exquisitely soft, my paws had pink pads, I knew I was beautiful, but I wasn't sure if this was right for me. Was I good enough for Gretel?

I didn't exactly have a choice.

Gretel looked at me silently for a moment, and then said, 'You are a darling, darling little Fuzzball.' I hoped that wasn't going to be my name, but then she turned to the cat lady and said, 'Can I have her? She's definitely THE ONE.'

I wanted to say goodbye to my brother, my only family now, but I was whisked into a luxurious carrier with pink fluff. A lot of fuss was going on. People saying, 'Oh, you are a lucky kitten,' and shuffling about with papers while I sat in there, lonely, and wanting my mother. I even wanted Harriet. We had spent a couple of nights cuddled up to the big dog who seemed to love us. She was warm and peaceful, her heartbeat so steady and slow. She'd even let us play with her silky ears and the tip of her tail. It helped me to make a decision: I wanted a dog in my life. A dog was a solid reliable friend.

Gretel was OK, but I was uneasy. Had I made the right decision? And I definitely didn't want to be called FUZZBALL.

Gretel's bungalow was fine. Warm and sweet-smelling, with soft carpets, a fur-lined cat bed with a roof, and a puss-flap leading to a sunny patio and a square of lawn. I should have been happy there, but I wasn't. It was lonely, even though Gretel made a fuss of me. She wanted me to be good.

I wasn't good. I was a BAD CAT.

My dad, Solomon, was the most saintly cat, and I wished he were there to teach me the mysteries and illogical rules about living with humans.

The first issue was the litter tray. I knew how to use it, but I didn't think it right to use it a second time. It was more creative to find some paper and make my own. I shredded a copy of the Damart catalogue before Gretel had read it, and she went ballistic.

'You wretched cat. Look at this STINK-ING mess. You're a bad girl. BAD GIRL,' and she grabbed my scruff like Jessica would have done and shook me. I was hurt and puzzled. It had been fun shredding the paper and making myself a luxurious heap behind the sofa and, when I'd used it, I'd carefully raked it up and covered it over. Problem solved.

I quickly became a compulsive paper shredder as I grew bigger. My new claws had to be kept sharp and it was a good workout. Gretel used to go out and shut the kitchen door so I couldn't go out through the puss-flap, and she'd always left a magazine some-where, by her bed or on a chair.

Next, I discovered the postman. I learned what time he came and recognised his foot-steps. Or I'd sit in the window, watching him pushing his trolley down the street, getting more and more excited as he approached. Once he was on the path, I shot into the hall and waited, tingling, by the front door. There were always catalogues in plastic that landed with a slap, but if they were heavy I ignored them. What I liked were the paper letters, especially the brown ones, which made a succulent tearing noise. In one part of my mind, I was being a lion ripping skin from its prey, and in another way, I was being creative and pragmatic while Gretel was out.

One morning, she came in the back door with her shopping bags and I ran to meet her like a cat should. She sat down and took me onto her lap, and I learned how to give her healing. She had pain in her joints; they used to glow in her aura like hotspots. I draped myself over her knees or up on her shoulder and practised the art of purring, which I had brought with me from the spirit world. It was a vibration that generated streams of minute stars that only I could see. But Gretel felt it. I knew she did.

'Oh, you are a darling cat. You're so good for me,' she said as we relaxed together. But as soon as she got up and went into the hall, it all changed.

'You BAD CAT,' she shouted when she saw the heaps of shredded paper I was so proud of. 'My LETTERS! You've ruined them.'

She seized me in angry hands and held me

up so that my face was close to hers, and hissed at me like a mother cat. 'WHAT am I going to DO with you, Fuzzball, eh?'

I hated being treated like that. I flattened my ears and lashed my tail. After all that healing, Gretel was abusing me! I kicked out with my back legs, and my claws were out. They caught in her clothes and scratched her neck.

'You little demon,' she snarled and dropped me. I mean – dropped me, not put me down nicely. Unprepared, I twisted and landed awkwardly. Stunned, I crouched there, looking up at her, hoping she'd apologise, pick me up and make peace with me. Instead, she clapped her hands right in my ear and I ran away, through the puss-flap and into the garden. It was lovely sunshine, but I sat in the dark underneath the decking and licked myself miserably. I was trembling inside with a mixture of fear and anger. What had I done? How could Gretel change so quickly from sweetness to rage?

I'd never felt so alone. I wanted my parents and my brothers to guide and comfort me. I wanted a dog like Harriet. I wanted a nice name, a beautiful romantic name suitable for a silver and white tabby who had come here to heal. My life wasn't working out the way

I'd planned.

Then I remembered my angel. It was a long time since I'd talked to her, and I'd never really learned how to see her on this planet. Where was she?

A cloud blew over the sun, the garden darkened and rain spattered down, splashing the leaves with drops. It dripped through cracks in the decking and I shrank back against the wall, feeling worse.

The storm was soon over and the sun shone out again, making everything glisten, and tempting me out to feel it on my fur. I sat on the path and stared out at a bright raindrop hanging from a leaf. The sunlight was turning it into a blazing star, so bright I squinted my eyes to look at it, and it started turning pink, then gold, then blue. As I turned my head sideways, the rays of light revolved like the spokes of a wheel.

Mesmerised, I focused on the centre where the rays of pink, gold and blue converged, and with my daydream came a memory from the spirit world. That magic dot in the centre was the point of infinity. In my mind, I could go through it, into the land of spirit. Ignoring everything else around me, ignoring my hurt feelings, I concentrated on it. I zoomed in, slipped through it into a place of light.

And there, waiting for me, was my fantastic angel. The Angel of Secrets. Her colours were those of a dragonfly in the sun, her face was the happiest beaming smile, welcoming me. Just seeing her gave me courage.

'It's all going wrong, living with Gretel,' I confided. 'She's so angry with me for being a cat.'

'I know, I know. I see it all,' my angel said, and she wrapped her light around me. I nestled into the sparkles, and listened.

'It's a time of learning,' she explained. 'You are a young cat with no mother to teach you. Gretel is teaching you how to live with humans. If you don't learn this, you will suffer all your life.'

'But why can't she teach me nicely?' I asked.

'She doesn't know how. She's a human. She has stuff to learn too.'

'But why am I a bad cat?'

My angel threw an extra whoosh of stars around me, warming my soul. 'You're not a bad cat. There are no bad cats. You must forgive Gretel. She doesn't know a better way, and she was treated unkindly by her family. When she is fierce, she is afraid.'

I cuddled into the warmth of her aura as if it were a cushion.

'Your mother, Jessica, was a very creative cat. She did all the things you are doing now and got punished and called a demon for it. But she was loyal and courageous too.'

'But this isn't how my life is meant to be,' I said. 'I'm not meant to be with Gretel, am I? And I'm not "Fuzzball".' I flicked my tail in frustration.

'You are an earth kitten. All young earthlings must go through a time of learning, and if you don't learn, you can't move on,' said my angel. 'So learn! Learn what Gretel is trying to teach you. We have work for you.'

She melted back into the light, leaving me realising I was staring at a sparkle on a raindrop. I sat thinking about how to please Gretel. Catch a mouse and present it to her? Or that robin who was tugging a worm out of the lawn. He'd make a nice gift for Gretel.

I stalked him, and pounced, but he flew up, muttering, and swore at me from the rooftop. And he'd lost his worm.

Full of energy and frustration, I rioted in the garden, rehearsing pounces and charges, and playing wildly with a soft ball Gretel had hung from a string for me. Then I heard laughter, and she came out and sat by the lily pond, watching me.

'You must forgive Gretel,' the angel had

42

said, so I gave it a go, rubbing my silky fur against her legs and smiling up at her. I gazed right into her soul and saw that she did need forgiveness and lots of it. Behind that powdered exterior was a person who carried a burden and didn't know how to let go of it.

'Oh, Fuzzball. Come on then.' She patted her lap and I jumped up and made a fuss of her, kissing and purring and kneading her with soft paws. 'You've forgiven me,' she said, and we were friends again. Phew!

But it didn't end there. The same thing happened repeatedly through the autumn as I tried to understand what I did to make Gretel lose her temper and call me a demon. It came to a head just before Christmas.

I was almost fully grown but still loving to play. One dark afternoon, Gretel came home with a tree. A spiky fir tree in a red pot. I was sleepy, curled up in a chair, but I sat up to watch what she was doing. She opened a box full of shiny baubles and funny little creatures on loops of string, and she hung them all over the tree.

'There. Our Christmas tree, Fuzzball. Isn't it pretty?'

She switched on some lights and the tree twinkled like magic. We sat in the dark

43

admiring it. The tree was hypnotic. I couldn't stop looking and longing to leap up and play with all those things. There was a miniature white teddy bear with a bobble hat, there was a fat little man in a red coat and his face looked so real. It had glittery eyes. There was a skinny fairy right at the top, looking very serious. And, hey, there was a BIRD on the tree, a robin like the one in the garden. He looked at me cheekily, but was he real? I couldn't work it out.

I jumped down and stalked round the tree, looking at that robin from all angles. The shiny baubles attracted me too and I sat in front of one, fascinated to see a tiny cat inside, a cat that moved when I moved. There was a room in there with a window and a fire burning. Could it be a mirror? I peered behind it, but it was perfectly round, a ball on a string. Gretel must have hung it there for me to play with. I patted it experimentally, and the whole tree shivered and shook and glittered in new places.

'NO,' said Gretel in that warning kind of voice I hated.

I looked at her and her aura had spikes.

'Fuzzball! NO. You are not to play with the Christmas tree.'

By now, I knew what NO meant. My back

and tail twitched with irritation. Didn't cats have any rights? Why couldn't I play and be joyful? Turning my back on Gretel, I sat in the doorway pretending to wash.

'Good girl,' she said, but I ignored that. I knew I was going to play with that Christmas tree when the opportunity came. I dreamed about it all night and, in the morning, I curled up in my favourite chair and pretended to be asleep. Gretel came and looked at me, her car keys jingling, but I didn't move, even when she stroked me softly and told me she was going to fetch her mother.

I listened to the engine of her neat little blue car, and the slam of the garage door. She had gone. I got up and flexed my muscles, ate some of the mashed sardine she'd left for me, and swanned into the lounge.

The Christmas tree was still there, glittering expectantly, and now it was mine. Fantastic bubbly joy filled my heart; I was so happy, and I wanted that feeling to last. So I moved in slowly on the tree, my eyes chasing its moving points of light. I chose a pink shiny bauble and messed about, touching noses with my reflection. I patted it and watched everything shake and settle down again. There was a wild feeling deep in my being, charging me up like an electric cat.

A few more swipes from my paw, and the pink bauble was off the tree. I chased it across the floor, under the chair and out again. It rolled under the sideboard and wouldn't come out. So I swiped another one down and batted it into the kitchen, where it went ping-pinging across the tiles.

I leaped and twirled, and belted round and round the tree in a frenzy of fun, swiping more and more baubles until they were scattered everywhere. I chased them north, south, east and west, skidding and pouncing and tearing the carpet with my claws. I got the miniature white teddy bear down, carried him in my mouth into Gretel's bedroom, and pushed him into the toe of one of her slippers, thinking I'd have another game later getting him out.

The fat Father Christmas went under the sofa where my collection of secret comfort toys was hidden – my catnip mouse, a Babybel cheese, and various bits and pieces from the garden. With my heart beating very fast, I sat for a moment, looking up at the tree. A few smaller baubles were left at the top with the skinny fairy. I didn't fancy her but I wanted that robin SO much.

The only way to catch him was to leap high into the prickly branches. It was hard, but the challenge fired me up even more. I leaped until my fur felt on fire, my paws hot and tingling. At last, I had the robin between my paws, in mid-air, and I wasn't going to let go. I fell backwards and the tree toppled right over, spilling earth on Gretel's pink carpet, and I had to crawl out from under it, the toy robin in my mouth, my heart thudding with excitement.

It had been a wonderful morning and, worn out, I took the robin onto the window-sill behind the curtain. I tucked my paws under myself and went blissfully to sleep with my chin on it.

Hours later, Gretel pushed open the back door and dumped her shopping on the table. There was a crunching, cracking sound. Still sleepy, I stayed behind the curtain.

'What's that doing here?' she shrieked.

'Looks like a bauble off the tree,' said another voice, an old quavery sort of voice. 'And you've trodden on it. Where's the dustpan?'

'Don't fuss, Mum. I'll sweep it up in a minute.'

I listened in growing alarm as Gretel came into the lounge and saw the wreckage.

'Oh, NO!' she howled. 'What an unbelievable mess.'

Feeling the shockwaves, I stayed hidden behind the curtain. I was in terrible trouble.

'It's that CAT. That CAT's done this!'

'I told you not to have a cat, dear. I wouldn't have one.'

'How can ONE CAT make such an almighty mess?'

'You'll have to get that carpet steam-cleaned, dear.'

'I worked so hard to keep this place decent. The Christmas tree looked wonderful, and it's ruined ... RUINED.' Gretel began to make the most alarming howling noise. I listened in horror, thinking I should run to her and purr. I fluffed my fur, kinked my tail and padded out from behind the curtain with my face bright and friendly.

'There you are!' she screamed. 'You little BEAST of a cat. Look what you've done. Look at it.'

'Don't take on so, Gretel,' said her mother, but Gretel had only just started, and seeing me made her worse.

She grabbed me with bony hands, and chucked me out into the garden. It was freezing fog. I went to the puss-flap to come in again, but she had jammed it shut. I meowed and scrabbled but she banged her fist in the door and shouted.

'You're not coming in here, you demon cat. You're going back to that cat home. I'm not keeping you any longer.'

'But she's such a lovely cat.' Gretel's mother professed not to like cats, but she was defending me. I sat outside in the fog, listening to the loud conversation and the sweeping, tinkling sounds from the kitchen. Then Gretel's mother said, 'Can't she live in the shed? When I was a girl, our cats lived outside.'

'Today's cats don't.'

'Well, she's got to go somewhere. It's Christmas.'

'I do know that.'

In the end, Gretel did try to put me in the shed. She set up a cardboard box with a rug in it, while I purred round her ankles, trying to make peace. She put me in it and I jumped out immediately. I didn't like that rug. It felt bad and scratchy, as if a bad-tempered person had used it and left their anger in every fibre of the wool. And the box smelled of vinegar.

I didn't want to be in the shed. It was cold and dusty, and there were fierce-looking tools on the walls, and no space for me to play, and no fire to warm my bones. Gretel had left the window open so that I could come and go, and the freezing fog drifted in, making everything damp. It was my first Christmas, and I was so lonely and miserable. I meowed and meowed through the night at the sealed-up puss-flap. Eventually, Gretel opened the door in her dressing gown, and I shot past her ankles, headed for the rug by the fire.

'Oh no you don't.' She picked me up. 'You are driving me UP THE WALL. Meowing all night, keeping me awake.'

I tried to be loving and friendly, but she ignored my love and carried me out to the shed again. She shut the window, and the door.

I was a prisoner.

'It could be a blessing,' said my angel. 'Wait and see.'

She was right in a way. Gretel eventually melted and let me back into the bungalow. But I was never left in there alone again, and, when she went out, she left me in the shed, if she could find me. I got wise to it and hid, so when she did go out, I had freedom to explore.

And that was how I came to be sitting on the wall on a summer evening when Tammy-Lee walked by and my angel said, 'Follow that girl.'

Chapter Three

A BABY CALLED ROCKY

The experience of being out all night was new to me. I'd never seen the stars before, or watched the dawn. The sun didn't snap on like a lamp, but took its time. Once, I had sat and watched a water lily opening on Gretel's pond, and it was like that – slow and pink, unfurling petals across the sky until it exposed the centre disc of burning yellow. The burr of moths' wings on the scented elderflowers was replaced by the hum of bees, and above me on the top branch, a blackbird started singing. I listened and absorbed his pure melody into my heart. So that's what birds were about. Pure joy.

When I got up for a stretch, the blackbird changed his song to a harsh whit-whitting alarm call, warning the other birds that I was there.

I was hungry for my breakfast, and needed to move, but when I did, the baby boy started to cry. I ran back and kissed his tiny red nose and he opened his eyes. They were the brightest turquoise blue, and full of astonishment. He responded to my purring with a sort of chuckle, and I arranged myself over him again, keeping him warm. I nudged his arm with my head, trying to get him to stroke me, but it felt floppy and weak. Was he dying? His aura was thin now, just a fuzzy line of aqua and lemon. His angel was there, and she was a rainbow swirl in the air.

The baby gave little grizzling cries, intermittently, but the crying seemed to suck the remaining energy out of him. All I could do was watch over him and purr. He needed a human. He needed food and milk, but he couldn't crawl out and help himself. I had to find someone, or he would die.

Anxiously, I watched the common from under the canopy of elder trees, and in the distance people were walking their dogs. But no one came past the elder tree.

I listened to the burble of the river rushing over stones, and at last I heard footsteps clonking over the bridge. Shoes. Like TammyLee. Had she come back?

I bounded out with my tail up, and saw a woman with a scrap of a dog on a lead. It flew into a frenzy of yapping when it saw me, but I wasn't fazed. Then it cowered and wound its lead round her ankles as I approached.

'Well, you're a brave cat,' she said, bending down to stroke me, 'and aren't you beautiful! I hope you're not lost.'

I meowed and meowed, sitting on the path in front of her. If only the baby would cry. What could I do? She stood there, watching me, the dog tucked under her arm. He was twitching his nose and looking towards the tree.

'Come on, puss, I've gotta go home.'

She stepped over me, and walked on. I ran after her, meowing. I belted past her, with my tail fluffed out, and again sat on the path in front of her. I lifted my paw and patted the hem of her coat, then got it between my teeth and pulled.

'What ARE you doing?' She laughed at me. 'You funny cat.'

I did the loudest meow ever. It echoed over the common, and I trotted back towards the tree, stopped and turned to look at her. She frowned, and just then, magically, the baby boy gave that little grizzling cry.

Still with the dog tucked under her arm, she followed me under the tree. She saw the bag. She looked in.

'Oh my God. Oh no, NO. A baby. Oh, you poor little MITE.'

I thought she would pick him up straight away, but instead, she tied the dog to a tree, and jumbled in her bag. She took out a mobile phone, tapped it and did a lot of talking. 'I'm Linda Evans, and I'm on the common by the footbridge over the river, and I've found an abandoned baby. He looks new-born, and he's been dumped in a carrier bag. He needs medical attention, and so does the mother, whoever she is.'

Next, Linda eased the baby out of the bag. He was so small, smaller than me, and I was a cat.

'Look what he's wrapped in,' she exclaimed, pulling at a thin purple scarf with threads of silver in it. She cuddled the baby close and wrapped her coat around him. 'You poor dear little soul. Who's done this to you?' Tears ran down her cheeks, and the dog was whimpering. I went and sat beside it firmly, to calm it down, but its legs went on shivering.

Linda seemed to get into a panic as she watched the baby. She sat down on the grass with him on her lap.

'Don't die on me, darling. Come on.' She rocked him and cuddled him, but he was still and floppy. Holding the phone again, she shouted, 'Be quick. He's not going to

54

make it. Please. Please get here.'

She pulled out a scrap of torn paper from the folds of the scarf, and looked at it. Four words were scrawled on it in bright pink letters.

'*HIS NAME IS ROCKY,*' Linda said, showing me the words on the paper as if I could read. She pursed her lips. 'That's all,' she said. 'That's all his mum left with him. Evil woman, whoever she is. Just give me five minutes with her. Doing that to a dear little defenceless baby.'

I ran back to her and added my purring and my love, and she didn't push me away. A siren was screaming up the road on the other side of the river, a blue light flashing. I climbed up into the elderberry tree, to watch what happened. Oh, those humans were awesome. They pounded across the bridge, dressed in orange, a man and a woman, leaving the ambulance with its light flashing, its doors open. They took the baby boy and rushed him inside the ambulance, where they messed about with tubes and bottles, working on this tiny being called Rocky, whose life I had saved.

From my perch in the tree, I could see that his aura suddenly brightened, and he cried then, properly. The paramedic turned and gave a thumbs up, and Linda scooped up her dog and burst into tears.

'Will you stay there, please? The police are on their way.'

The doors of the ambulance were closed and it raced off. I watched it go, remembering the baby's bright blue eyes, remembering his soul energy.

I hung around, making friends with Linda as she waited there, crying, a screwed-up tissue in her hand. She seemed glad to have me with her. I worked my way up to her broad shoulder and draped myself over it.

'You are a loving cat,' she said, and looked into my eyes as I peeped round at her. She was a motherly person, like Harriet, I thought. Yes, Linda was a Labrador kind of human. We had a bond now. We'd both helped to save the life of an abandoned baby.

When the police arrived, I stayed on Linda's shoulder while they talked, and they were interested in me.

'So what's the cat doing here?' the policeman asked. 'Is it your cat?'

'No ... but it led me to the baby. Just like a dog would have done.'

Me! Like a dog? I was miffed at that.

'Perhaps the cat belongs to the mother. Has it got a collar?'

'No.' Linda burrowed her fingers in my ruff. 'It's a well-cared-for cat, that's obvious.'

'Have you ever seen it before?'

'No. Never. But I don't think it's a stray, and it's not feral.'

'If it's microchipped, it might lead us to the mother. Let me hold it.' The policeman held out his arms and lifted me gently off Linda's neck. I'd never had a cuddle with a policeman before so I touched noses with him and made a fuss, purring and rubbing and kissing his neck, and he was enjoying it, I could tell. He was feeling my back to see if I'd got a microchip, whatever that was.

'I think I can feel one. We should definitely hang on to this cat and get it scanned.'

He was holding me too tightly now. I knew what he was planning to do. I could feel the intention buzzing through his fingers. He was going to put me in one of those baskets. I had to act fast.

Without giving him any warning, I went from being a loving softie to a fighting tiger. I kicked hard with my back legs, thrashed my body around, and managed to reverse out of his grasp, a long thread of police uniform caught in my claw. I hit the ground, bounded, and fled, my tail kinked cheekily.

'Follow it, will you!'

The other policeman thundered after me across the common. I was fast, and smart. His boots crashed through the bushes but I soon evaded him, diving into some nettles, up a fence and into a garden, over a garage roof and into the street. Through the front gardens again, I ran stretched out like a fox with my tail streaming. A few dogs barked at me, and blackbirds flew up from lawns as I escaped into the town.

Satisfied, I sat on a busy corner, watching the traffic and the children going to school, and wondering where my home was. I didn't know. None of the roads looked familiar. I couldn't locate any of the scent marks I had left as I followed TammyLee.

Being lost didn't faze me. There were so many nice people around, and the town looked interesting with its bright windows and lovely smells of bacon and toast. Intrigued, I trotted down the busy road, pausing to sharpen my claws on the magnificent lime trees.

I crossed the road with a bunch of children and a bleeping noise, and the cars magically stopped in a neat line. For me? I heard laughing, and people saying, 'Look at that cat.' But when I sat down to wash my face in the middle of the crossing, the bleeping stopped, someone screamed, and a young man bounded into the road, picked me up and carried me the rest of the way.

'Stupid cat!' he said, and I flicked my tail in annoyance, and the traffic made a terrible noise, blowing horns and swearing.

'Keep that bloody cat off the road.'

'It's not my cat,' yelled the young man.

I jumped up onto a massive flower pot full of pansies, and sat there to wash my face. It had to be done. But humans don't understand what it's like to have fur and the need to keep on washing it. And why not sit somewhere pleasant like in the middle of a pot of yellow and purple pansies? They were scented and had wistful faces like kittens. I must have looked beautiful there in the morning sun.

'Get off, cat!' A woman who looked like a bulldog gnashed her teeth at me. 'You're squashing the flowers.'

I stared at her. Obviously, she didn't know I'd just saved a baby's life.

'Aw, leave him,' said a kinder one.

'Him!' I thought, indignantly.

I settled down to wash in the lovely pansy pot.

Next, I followed some people into a shopping mall and had a mad half hour on the slippery floor. It was like a skating rink for cats. I twirled and skidded, figuring out how fast I had to run to slide a long way on my belly. After the night of guarding the tiny baby, it felt amazing to be having fun and making people laugh. I chased a paper cup down the mall, under benches and into doorways. I pretended it was a mouse and hid round a corner, then pounced on it, and skidded.

When I was tired, I strolled down to the pavement café and arranged myself on a chair, and the couple who were eating breakfast there gave me some crisp curls of bacon and corners of buttery toast. I padded round the tables with my tail up, and was given a saucer of warm milk, some bits of sausage and a kipper's tail, before the staff noticed me.

'We don't encourage cats,' said the waiter, hovering over me with an armful of plates. 'Go on. Shoo!' He stamped his foot and hissed at me, and the plates slipped alarmingly.

My hunger satisfied, though, I walked on down the shopping mall. I went into a clothes shop and swung from a rail of T-shirts, pulling them onto the floor.

'OUT!' shouted the shop assistant, and

she ran at me clapping her hands. 'You're wrecking the place, you shouldn't be in here, you crazy cat.'

Miffed, I walked on with my tail waving elegantly, and into the shop next door, which was full of televisions. And there I had the shock of my life.

I was on television ... well, on a whole shop full of televisions in different sizes. I sat down in front of a big one that made me look like an enormous fluffy tiger on Linda's shoulder.

'The baby was discovered by this woman, Linda Evans, who was walking her dog.' Now the picture was of a reporter lady sitting on a red sofa.

Then I sat up even straighter. There was the tiny baby, Rocky, in the arms of a nurse. He'd got a little white hat on and a blanket wrapped round him, but I could see the mole on his cheek and the glint of astonishment in his turquoise eyes. It was definitely him. My baby. My Rocky.

I went up to the screen, to touch noses with him, patted it and jumped back, not liking the crackle of static through my fur. I couldn't stop looking at Rocky and wherever I looked, he was there on every screen, and people were walking past the shop, ignoring him.

'We are hoping his mother will come forward,' the nurse was saying. 'She may need medical help, and Rocky needs his mum. He's a dear little chap.'

Then they showed me – again! – and the policeman who'd tried to hold me, and he was saying, 'If anyone sees this cat or knows where it lives, please get in touch with us. There could be a connection.'

I knew who Rocky's mother was. TammyLee. How could a cat give that information? But even if I'd been able to talk, I wouldn't have told. It was a secret I shared only with TammyLee. We had been drawn to each other, I had felt her sadness, and she had called me 'magic puss cat'. TammyLee and I were soul mates.

I had to find her. The time had come for me to grow up, stop playing, and work. I'd search to the ends of the earth for TammyLee.

But just as I was making this momentous decision, a man's voice shouted, 'THAT'S THE CAT!' An agile young man, who'd spotted me watching myself on TV bounded to the shop doors and slammed them shut.

And I was a prisoner. Again.

Chapter Four

A HOT CAR

I searched the shop for an escape route, but there wasn't one.

'You stand there,' Dave the manager called to his mate.

Both wore smart white shirts, like tuxedo cats, black trousers and shiny shoes. Obviously, they weren't used to cats, it made me nervous, but my angel's voice rang in my aura, keeping me calm and still. Self-control was something I needed to work on. It was hard. My instinct was buzzing like a bee, telling me to run wild in the shop and not be caught.

'Get it some milk from the back, Kyle,' said Dave. 'Shut it in the kitchen and we'll call the cops. Bit of free publicity, eh?'

There was no way out. A quick look around the walls and ceiling told me that. So I had to be pragmatic and trust these two young men, Dave and Kyle. I could see that Kyle had a fiery intelligence as he warily approached me, so I was polite, standing up and putting my tail up. A silent meow and eye contact had him transfixed in seconds. Gingerly, he picked me up, and airlifted me into the kitchen, kicking the door shut.

'Got him!' he shouted. 'You can open the shop now, Dave.'

Why did everyone think I was male?

Kyle stood with his back to the kitchen door, brushing my fluff from his black trousers and watching me lapping the milk he had given me. I'd hardly got room for it after my street-café breakfast. I was fine until the police turned up with a cat cage. Then I panicked in the small kitchen and squeezed myself behind the fridge.

'Come on, darling. It's all right. We're only going to scan you and take you home. Come on, my lovely.'

I didn't like it behind the fridge, so eventually, the policewoman's honeyed tones coaxed me out and into the cage where she'd hidden some cat treats and, hey, a cat-nip mouse. She kept talking to me kindly.

Bad memories of being a tiny kitten in one of those cages haunted me, so I kept still and quiet as I was carried into a police car and driven away with the blue light flashing. I thought about the friends I had made. The couple who had fed me at the street café, the lady who'd let me sit in the pansy pot, the young man who'd risked his life to get me off the road. In my search for Tammy-Lee, I planned to return to that shopping mall, and see my new friends. A cat who is alone and searching needs the support of friends.

It turned out that I *had* got a 'microchip', and the police took me home to Gretel, even though I didn't want to go.

Since the Christmas tree disaster, Gretel had changed her mind and decided she did want to keep me. She still shut me in the shed, usually with the window open to give me access to the garden. I used those times of freedom to roam the streets looking for TammyLee. I sat on the wall and waited for her to walk past, but she never did. I followed groups of children to school and sat watching the playground, but TammyLee was never there, and no one spoke her name. She seemed to have vanished.

Living with Gretel wasn't working. I tried to love her, but it wasn't easy. She loved me only when I was good and boring, not when I ran up the curtains or swung from the birch tree in the garden, or caught the orange fish from the lily pond. But she did teach me stuff that turned out to be useful, like going in the car. Instead of shutting me in the shed, she took to putting me in the car and taking me with her. At first I was petrified. But I soon got used to it. The car was warm and comfortable, and Gretel had set it up with a wire grill to stop me going into the front while she was driving, a cosy cat igloo where I could hide, and even some toys for me to play with. She talked to me a lot while we were going along, and sang me songs and played the radio. The trips were interesting. I learned to recognise places. Corners and buildings and parks. Even the shopping mall and the river bridge where TammyLee had stood with baby Rocky. I glimpsed the elder tree where I'd spent the night guarding him, and I sensed the wild country beyond the town, which I longed to explore.

So I became a car cat. I quite enjoyed it. Until one terrible day that changed my life.

It was a summer day, many weeks after I'd found the abandoned baby. The weather was so hot that it hurt my paws to walk on the patio. I was rolling on my back on the lawn, enjoying the sun on my belly and dabbing at passing flies.

'Come on, Fuzzball.' Gretel appeared in a

flimsy blue dress, twiddling her car keys. 'We'll go to the supermarket. At least they've got air conditioning in there.'

If I'd known what was going to happen, I'd never have let her pick me up, tuck me under her arm and put me in the car. It was hot in there, but she drove along with the window open. Lovely, except for the smell of a crowded town, the exhaust flumes, lawns being mown, the bakeries and the pubs. Far away was the briny tang of the river and the heather-covered moorland beyond the town, a scent on the wind that stirred a deep ancestral longing in me. Being a domestic cat was OK, but I had a wild streak in me that wasn't satisfied with fluffy cat beds and cat-nip mice.

There was a bad atmosphere in town. A sense of something simmering, about to erupt. People looked knocked out by the heat. Children were crying and dogs were being dragged along on leads on the hot pavements.

'I'll bring you an ice cream,' said Gretel, turning into the supermarket car park. She found a parking space, shut the windows and got out. 'I won't be long, Fuzzball.'

I sighed and settled down for a snooze. Used to being left in the car, I curled up, wrapped my tail around myself and closed my eyes.

Within minutes I was too hot. It wasn't like lying by the fire and having to move away from the heat. I was trapped in it, and suddenly I couldn't breathe. Alarmed, I climbed up onto the back of the seats, but it was worse up there near the roof of the car. Outside, the car roofs shimmered in the heat, dazzling me. I wanted to shut my eyes, but I was frightened. I clawed at the window, hoping to open it and get some air. It was so hot I had to breathe with my mouth open like a dog.

I longed for water but Gretel hadn't left me any. Desperately, I licked a few drops of condensation from the window glass, then worked my way round each of the windows, licking what moisture I could find, and all the time getting hotter and hotter.

There was no way of cooling myself down. I tore at my thick fur, trying to get some air on my skin, but nothing worked. I dug and scrabbled at the floor of the car, trying to find a hole or a crack I could make bigger with my teeth and claws. Soon my feet were burning, my claw sheaths sore, and my throat so dry. I was being dried up, cooked alive in that oven of a car.

Where was my angel? Where was she?

I listened. I kept still and called her name in my heart. The Angel of Secrets. Angel of Secrets. Angel... I was giddy now, and her voice came to me from far away. My body was collapsing and I just lay there panting. All I could hear was the alarming echo of my heartbeat, the rasp of my breath, and the distant whisper of her voice, repeating over and over again, 'Don't give up. Don't give up. Meow and someone will come. Meow. You must meow.'

I fought to stay awake, but I was losing consciousness, sinking into a boiling black darkness. I did meow, and it was loud, and painful. Yet my body seemed to take over and meow by itself, draining my last dregs of energy, calling, calling for help.

As I finally lost consciousness, I saw a face looking through the glass at me, and it wasn't Gretel.

I drifted through the dark, and reached the shoreline of the spirit world. A high fence of the brightest gold sent out beams of light spangled with pinpoints of intense colour. I sat before it and gazed through into the world I had loved so much, the spirit world where I was the Queen of Cats. Telepathically, I begged for the golden fence to open and let me through, let me go home, let me leave this body of pain lying in the hot car.

The voices I heard were muddled.

'Come back, Queen of Cats. You still have work to do.' That was my angel, and from beyond the golden fence I could hear purring. Loud, vibrational purring from the shining cats who had purred with me in the spirit world. They weren't welcoming me, but sending me back, floating on a carpet of purring.

I drifted back to the sound of human voices around the car. Someone saying, 'That poor cat in there!' and 'We have to get it out. NOW!'

My world exploded with a bang. A storm of broken glass scattered over me, into my fur and all over the car. Dazed, I saw the emerald green of the broken pieces. The air rushed in, and a pair of long arms reached through the hole in the window. I felt my limp body being lifted out.

'I've got him.'

'He's dead, isn't he?'

'Not quite. And it's a she cat. She's beautiful.'

Someone ran with me to the shade of a big plane tree and laid me on a bench. I felt the slats of wood under me, and the deliciously

70

cool canopy of the great tree. But I couldn't move. My breathing was laboured, my eyes wouldn't shut, and I was salivating.

'There's no time to get her to a vet.'

'Water. Get some water from the shopping bag.'

I heard running feet again, then the rustle of plastic and the soft pop of a bottle being opened. I hate water, but they were pouring it over me! It trickled round my neck, into my fur, along my back, over my parched face. I licked the drops and felt the healing cool of it soaking my hot body.

'Frozen peas,' said the voice. 'Bottom of the bag.'

More rustling, and something achingly cold and knobbly was put close to my back. My breathing eased a bit. I was coming alive again, coming back from my trip to the shorelines of the spirit world, reclaiming my beautiful silver tabby and white body.

'She's still breathing.'

'Come on, darling – it's all right.'

Didn't I know that voice? I focused my eyes and saw the lovely policewoman who had coaxed me into the cat cage and taken me home that day. I was glad, and disappointed too. I'd hoped it might be TammyLee.

My eyes were burning and they wouldn't

71

shut. I tried to sit up, but my legs wouldn't move. Yet I knew I wasn't dying. I'd come back into my beautiful cat body, my long silver tabby fur, my white socks and pink paws, my lovely tail. But none of it would move. I could feel it twitching, but I'd somehow lost control. It was scary. How could I play and live my life? I didn't want to be useless and immobile. I felt terribly afraid.

I wanted peace, and recovery time.

But it wasn't peaceful.

A crowd had gathered, looking at me as I lay on the bench, still gasping for breath and twitching. A row was breaking out. I heard Gretel's shriek of a voice and she was part of the row.

'My car,' she cried. 'It's been broken into.'

'Never mind your car,' a man was shouting at Gretel. 'Is this your cat? Look at the state it's in!'

I felt the old familiar shockwaves coming from Gretel as she saw me there on the bench, and I couldn't get up. I couldn't put my tail up and run to reassure her. She was under attack. People were shouting at her furiously.

'How could you leave a cat shut in a car in this heat?'

'Haven't you got any more sense?'

'Don't you CARE about your lovely cat?'

Gretel was crying and crying. 'Is she going to die? I didn't know. I didn't mean to.'

No one was being kind to Gretel. The shouting got even louder.

'I'm reporting you to the RSPCA, and you'll never keep an animal again. You CRUEL woman.'

'But is she dying?' Gretel kept asking. 'I'll take her to the vet's.'

'You won't. It's too late for that. If we hadn't been here, she'd be dead right now. Poor, poor cat. She's suffered so much.' Now the other person was crying, and I lay there, shuddering in the middle of it.

'I'll see that you pay for this. That cat will be taken away from you. You've no business keeping an animal.'

'It's disgusting.'

'But I do love her. She's called...'

Gretel didn't get the chance to say Fuzz-ball, and I was grateful for that. The lovely policewoman with the blonde ponytail intervened.

'Please calm down,' she kept saying firmly. 'The cat needs some quiet. Please!'

I felt Gretel slump down on the bench beside me, and she touched my wet fur gently. 'I'm sorry. I'm so, so sorry,' she wept, and I wanted to tell her it was OK, I'd for-given her, but I couldn't even lift my head to look at her. I knew I'd never see her again, and I wanted to say thank you to her for giving me a home and a fluffy cat bed, and all that food. The toys and the quiet even-ings on her lap by the fire. I wished those people would stop attacking her.

'Here's the animal ambulance. Move back please,' said the lovely policewoman, and I heard people shuffling back as a vehicle drove up. After that it went quiet and I heard the soft pattering of the plane-tree leaves above me.

The voices became murmurs and I was picked up and carried, my tail and legs floppy, into a silent and beautifully cool van with a blissfully soft bed inside. A kind man with a bright light around him sat beside me and kept trying to put my head inside a weird-looking cup of clear plastic.

'Come on, sweetheart. Come on, breathe. It's oxygen. Come on, try it. It's good stuff.'

He didn't hurt me, but held my head firmly, and I picked up on his thoughts. He wanted me to breathe a special kind of air that was inside the cup. I tried it, and it was cool and sweet. I couldn't get enough of it. This clear, pure, mysterious air he called oxygen was filling my body with the fizz of new life.

I was alive, but I still couldn't move. I took a last look at Gretel's tear-stained face looking in at me as they closed the doors. I felt the van driving away, with me in it, lying there, a useless dysfunctional wreck of a cat.

What would become of me now?

Chapter Five

AN ANIMAL HEALER

I didn't know what was going to happen next, but my life with Gretel was over. For long days and nights, I lay in the animal hospital on a white bed with a light in the roof, listening to the whimpering and wailing from other cats and dogs who were stretched out in recovery beds in that place.

The humans looked after me beautifully, and stroked me a lot, but their talk was gloomy.

'This cat is borderline,' I heard the man saying. 'We don't know what long-term effects the heat stroke will have. She could suffer from multiple organ failure and have to be put down. A pity. She's only a young cat.'

Every day they stuck a sharp needle in me and, yes, they took some of my blood! I could see it in the syringe. Then they put something in through another needle, and I felt better afterwards. Clever stuff. But I knew what I needed, and it wasn't available.

'What's happening to me?' I asked my angel.

'It's a window,' she replied.

'A window?'

'A time of waiting, a time of transition between two life times.'

'Am I going to die?'

'Not quite,' she said. 'But you are like a cat sitting in the window, watching what is outside. You can't move on to the new life we have planned for you until you help yourself to get better. You will need to be a strong healthy cat to cope with what is ahead.'

'Help myself!' I was surprised. I thought I could just lie there and let the humans work their mysterious magic with those needles and tubes.

'All the purring and the medicine can't make you right again,' said my angel. 'You need to HELP YOURSELF to find the healing you know you need.'

76

How could I FIND anything? I was lying flat in an animal hospital. Angels can be so unreasonable, I thought, and twitched my back and tail. My paws quivered in frustration. I stretched each of my front paws, splaying my toes and letting my claws curl out, then in again. Bits of me were working. It seemed a good time to wash, so I lifted each paw to my mouth and began licking and brushing my pink pads and the downy fur between my toes. It felt good.

'Oh, she's washing!' exclaimed one of the nurses who was walking past. She stopped by my cage. 'Good girl!' she said, like Gretel. Then the vet came and looked at me.

'I think we'll let Roxanne look at her later. Has she eaten anything?'

'Little bits. She still doesn't want to stand up.'

'But she's washing. That's a start.'

Later that day, the animal hospital went uncannily quiet. I wondered why. Then the main door opened and in came a girl in a blaze of light. Was she real? I stared, and found I could see a human in there, inside that blaze of light, just an ordinary lump of a girl with a long dark plait over one shoulder. I wanted her close to me, immediately. I couldn't wait.

My angel had told me to help myself, so I managed an echoing meow and at once the girl came to me and looked in with the most beautiful eyes.

'We thought you should start with the dogs, Roxanne,' said a nurse.

'No,' said Roxanne. 'This cat. She needs me now. She's right on the edge. I'll do her first.'

First. I was first! I meowed in welcome as Roxanne came right up to me, and the light from her aura flooded into my cage. She unlatched my door, and looked deeply into my eyes, like TammyLee had done.

'I'm Roxanne,' she whispered. 'I'm an animal healer, darling.'

As soon as I heard her voice and felt her touch, I wanted to cry, and I sort of did by sighing and making little mewling sounds in my throat.

'Is it OK to take her out?' Roxanne asked the nurse, who hovered beside us, watching and learning.

'Sure. She's not going anywhere. She's just laid there for days.'

Roxanne picked me up and sat down with me flopped on her lap.

'What's her name?' she asked.

'She hasn't got one.'

Again, Roxanne looked deep into my eyes. 'Then I shall give her one,' she said, 'it will come through to me.' I tingled all over. This girl of the blazing light was going to give me a name, a new, beautiful name, something I had longed for. I went on sighing and mewling, and with every sigh a stream of energy seemed to leave my body, as though my fur had been full of heavy dust weighing me down for all of my young life, and now, under Roxanne's healing touch, it was leaving.

I saw her hands, and they were full of colours as they moved over me. She went to my head first, and it felt like a soft cocoon of pure light was being woven around my skull, wrapping my face, my long whiskers, my ears, my nose.

'This cat is depressed,' Roxanne said to the nurse.

'Depressed!'

'Oh, yes, and deeply so. She's been hurt and it's never been healed. That's what is stopping her getting better.'

She knew. She'd looked into my soul. The relief was huge, it left my body in waves as her hands shone colours into me, deep emerald greens, hot white and glowing pink.

'That's it, darling. You let go of it all,' she whispered to me, and my emotional pain shuddered through me, and began to leave. I saw it all. The very first hurt of my mum cat not liking me, the terrible shock of Joe tipping us in the hedge like rubbish. Then Gretel. Calling me Fuzzball. Calling me a BAD CAT. Calling me a DEMON. Shutting me out in the freezing fog. Locking me in the shed. And then leaving me to die in a hot car.

Gretel hadn't meant to hurt me. She didn't understand. I'd forgiven her, every time, but the pain had burrowed into my mind and made me depressed. Now this wonderful animal healer, Roxanne, had chosen me – FIRST – and she knew what to do, what to whisper into my twitching ears. She wasn't in a hurry. She spent ages healing me, sending colours into every part of my body.

'You take as much as you need, darling,' she kept saying. And I did. I soaked up the colour and the healing energy like a starving soul. Gretel had stroked me and played with me, but no one had loved me like this. I felt I'd come home. I felt lighter and lighter, as if I were a thistle seed that could blow for miles in the sunshine.

Then I heard purring, and it was me. I was purring.

'And now – I'll give you your name,' said

Roxanne. I looked attentively into her shiny dark eyes and waited. 'You're very beautiful,' she said. 'Your fur has the colours of a water-fall in the sunlight: silver and black with a tinge of gold and snowy white. And when you are well you will leap and dance and run fast like the mountain streams. So I'll call you TALLULAH. It's Native American for "Leaping water".' She whispered this to me so softly, the words were like gossamer, precious and strong. I wasn't even sure whether I was hearing them or whether she was sending them by telepathy.

'TALLULAH.'

I was thrilled. I had a name. A beautiful name that was full of music, a name that honoured my beauty and made me feel good.

A buzz of happiness started inside me, and I rolled over and managed to sit up and purr my gratitude to Roxanne. I was determined to touch noses with her, and I stretched up, wobbling a bit on my legs, and kissed her glowing face.

I was healed.

I was a new cat.

I had become Tallulah.

Chapter Six

BEING TALLULAH

On the day I left the animal hospital, I saw the mountains for the first time. They were peacock blue against the sky beyond the town and I wondered why I'd never noticed them before. I studied them as we travelled along, through familiar streets, past the common and the elderberry tree where I had found Rocky. Dark berries hung from it now. It was late summer, still hot, but the car I was travelling in was airy and quiet.

Being Tallulah made me feel proud and excited. Not knowing where I was going didn't bother me. I couldn't wait to arrive and start my search for TammyLee.

The car followed the river out of town, past its foamy places and waterfalls as it flowed down from the hills. I longed to get out and sit watching them, seeing the colours of my fur as Roxanne had described them. Silver, black, tinges of gold and snowy white. I longed to climb trees, and explore, chase leaves through the woods, hide in the long grass, and stalk mice in the moonlight. I was a free spirit now. I was Tallulah.

'You must be patient for a while longer, Tallulah,' said my angel as we turned into a farm gateway and down a track to a cottage. Immediately, I could hear the cats. There were other cats there, and all of them meowing. I hoped they would like me.

But when the car stopped, I was again carried out in the cat basket. There was a lovely house, but we didn't go inside. Instead, we went round to a yard at the back, and along the wall was a line of wire enclosures, each with a cat inside. Cages. Prisons. What a let-down! I was put inside one, and it had double doors so that I couldn't escape when someone came in.

'Hello, my luvvy.'

A warm friendly woman welcomed me, and she smelled of cats. Her eyes sparkled at me. I meowed back.

'I'm Penny,' she told me, 'and I'm the cat lady, that's what everyone calls me. I'm not adopting you, luvvy, but fostering you, and you can live in this lovely Cat Protection pen until we find a super home for you.'

She came into the pen with me, and opened the door of my travelling basket. I stepped out politely, with my tail up and my whiskers shining in the morning sun.

'Tallulah,' said Penny thoughtfully. 'That's a nice name, and aren't you just BEAUTIFUL! We'll have no trouble finding you a nice home. You won't be here for long.'

She stayed in the pen with me, sitting on a chair while I explored my new home. It had some great perches I could climb up to and sit on. It had a little house with a window and a warm bed inside. There was a huge litter tray, and a post with rope wound round it and I spent some time smelling it. Judging by the claw marks, dozens of cats had used it as a claw-sharpener. In a box on the floor were some toys: a ball with a bell inside, a brand-new cat-nip mouse, a teddy bear and some other bits and pieces. I looked at them, but didn't yet feel like playing. When I'd inspected every inch of the pen and found no way out, I jumped onto Penny's lap and she stayed there for me, smoothing my long fur while I purred myself to sleep.

Eventually, she got up and tenderly put me on the chair.

'I'll be back to see you, my luvvy. We'll have lots of cuddles,' she said, but I jumped down and followed her to the gate, meowing as she gently pushed me back and closed it tightly.

Horrified, I ran round and round the pen, calling and meowing. Surely, I wasn't a prisoner! I was Tallulah. I had a right to enjoy the world, to charge across lawns with my tail streaming, to scale trees and hang from branches, to dive under bushes and pounce on people's feet. These humans who looked after me so well had taken from me what I most treasured – my freedom!

And how would I ever find TammyLee?

I sat by the gate, my nose to the crack where it would open, and then I waited, planning the speed of my escape, how fast I would dart out when it was opened. I looked out at the garden beyond, and the road winding away beside the river, and planned my escape route. I'd follow the river back into town, back to the bridge where TammyLee had left Rocky. She'd go back there, eventually, I was sure.

When Penny came back with a dish of food for me, I did slip past her ankles and out of the gate, only to find she had cleverly shut the first gate and I was still trapped. Distraught, I gazed up at Penny with my golden eyes and meowed piteously.

'Aw, you poor darling.' She picked me up but I wriggled out of her arms and ran to the gate. Penny came after me, stroking and talking to me in a lovely voice, letting me smell the delicious meat she had brought me. But I didn't want anything except my freedom. The need for it burned inside me, and I tried to convey it to Penny. She understood me, but she didn't do what I wanted. She didn't let me out.

Night came, and I was still distraught. I ran round and round. I climbed the high wire fence in every place, searching, hoping for a hole to escape through. But it was rigid. I meowed and zigzagged around until my paws were sore and so was my throat. By dawn, I was exhausted and crept into the warm bed, curled up and slept until mid-morning.

As soon as I heard Penny's voice, I tumbled out, in such a hurry to get to her and beg her to let me go. Please, please let me go.

Penny was in the next-door pen, cuddling and fussing a rather portly black tomcat who had watched me through the wire with a disapproving stare. He looked contented, and so did the ginger tomcat on the other side who was tucking into a juicy looking breakfast. I sniffed at my uneaten supper, which had gone dry and had flies buzzing round it. I ate a little bit, then jumped up to the higher perch to feel the sun on my fur and see the mountains.

It seemed a good time to wash.

Washing is a sort of ritual that stabilises cats. For me, it had become a time to think. I wanted Penny to explain to me why I was shut in, and for how long. So I sent her the thought, and when she did come into my pen, she sat down with me again. I stretched myself over her heart and reached up to pat her face with a long paw. I knew she loved cats, so why did she shut me in?

She looked at me thoughtfully, and I sent my question again with all the power of my golden eyes and another pat from my newly washed paw.

'I know,' she said. 'It's not much fun being shut in, is it, Tallulah?'

I encouraged her with a purr-meow and a kiss on the nose.

'You're a very beautiful and intelligent cat,' she said, talking to my soul. 'And someone will come and choose you – a good person who knows how to take care of a cat. We make sure of that. We don't let cats go to bad homes.' Her hands were stroking my neck and rubbing behind my ears and under my chin. 'It might be today,' she said. 'Or it might be tomorrow. Or it might be a long time, many dark nights. These two have been here for months, haven't you, my luvvies?' She pointed at the black cat and the ginger one, who were both washing and listening. 'But you've got to choose too, Tallulah. Don't go with someone you don't like.'

I stared at her, getting the firm tone, and the pictures she was sending me from her mind. Nice people coming to choose a cat. And I remembered. Gretel had chosen me. I'd been too small to resist. But this time it would be different, I was determined. Even if the people were nice, I wouldn't go with them if it felt wrong.

'I'll put you in the paper this week,' said Penny, and she took a photo of me with a silver camera, and showed it to me on a screen. I looked like the teeniest fairy of a cat in there, but I purred and touched noses with the image, and Penny laughed so loudly that the wire fences rattled and shook.

After that conversation, I settled down and accepted that I wouldn't be in the pen for long. I made the best use of the space, playing a lot and climbing and keeping my claws sharp. Two people came to see me the very next day, and I remembered Penny's advice. It was a hard thing for me to do but I turned my back on them and went all huffy, climbing up to the top perch and sitting there, washing. It worked.

'She's such a pretty cat, but I don't think she wants to go with us,' the lady said to Penny. I watched the ginger cat next to me, who was meowing loudly and scrabbling at the bars, looking up at the two people adoringly.

'He's too old, really.'

'And he's a tomcat.'

'But he loves you,' said Penny. 'Look at him, poor luvvy; he's been in that pen all summer. And he's got oodles of love to give.'

The ginger cat eventually got what he wanted. He made a fuss of the two people, and ran into the cat basket with his tail up. As they carried him away, he was kissing the bars and purring, and his eyes danced at me joyfully. I felt so lonely.

It got harder and harder as the days rolled by, and other cats came and went in the pens next to me. It got harder every time I saw one being taken home with 'nice people'. I wanted my freedom. I didn't want to get depressed again. No, I had come to this planet for a reason. I'd used up one of my nine lives and wasted my time with Gretel.

I seriously considered going with someone who wanted me, and then escaping, following the river back to TammyLee. My angel said no.

'Wait,' she kept telling me.

Penny told me she'd put my picture in the paper for a second time, and then something totally unexpected happened.

People didn't normally come in the mornings, so I was dozing in the sun, stretched out in the chair. I was used to hearing Penny's voice as she bustled around the cat pens, and I was so sleepy and comfortable that I didn't bother to open my eyes when I heard the click of the farm gate being opened.

Penny was patiently explaining something to someone who didn't want to listen.

'But I saw her in the paper. I know it's the right cat.'

'I understand that, my luvvy,' Penny was saying. 'But I can't allow you to take her today.'

'But why not? It's a perfectly good home for a cat. We've got a big garden. I've looked after lots of cats.'

'This is the Cat Protection League,' insisted Penny. 'And we don't home any of our cats until we've inspected the home they're going to.'

'You sound like you don't trust me.'

'Well, I don't know you, do I? I'm only doing my job, dear.'

'I thought you wanted a home for this cat.'

90

'Of course we do.'

'So I'm not good enough. Is that it?'

'I'm sure you are, dear. I just need to make sure – for the cat's sake.'

'I mean, what d'you think I'm gonna DO to her, for goodness' sake?'

'I'm sure you'll be fine, dear – but please.'

'Oh, yeah, yeah, I know.' The voice was getting higher and higher, even though Penny was keeping calm. There was something in the girl's voice that struck a chord in my memory. I'd been running along the top of a wall on a moonlit night. So much had happened to me since that night. It was hard to remember.

The footsteps and voices were coming nearer, walking down the side of the house. Soon, they would be round the corner and coming to the cat pens.

'Well, surely, I can at least LOOK at the cat,' came the girl's voice, and with it came a distinctive jingling sound that jogged my memory further. Bangles. An arm with gold and silver bangles on it.

By now, I was wide awake and sitting up in the chair. Penny knew I usually turned my back on people, not because I was rude, but because they weren't the right people for me. But this girl who was arguing so loudly with Penny – could it be ... could it be HER?

I tensed expectantly as they came round the corner together. When I saw the girl's aura of bright turquoise and lemon, I knew.

It was HER! My TammyLee!

I sailed down from the chair and ran across the pen with my tail flying like a plume. I flung myself at the fence and scrabbled with my paws, and meowed so loudly that it echoed off the stone walls of the farm. I wasn't going to make a mistake this time. My TammyLee had come for me. She'd found me. She wanted me.

I weaved from side to side as I waited for them to open the gates and come in.

'Well, well, well!' said Penny, and she reached down to pick me up, but I twisted away from her and stared up at TammyLee with my golden eyes.

She gasped, and held out her arms. I leaped straight up and she caught me, her bangles jingling and tinkling. She looked into my soul with eyes that were green as clover leaves. And then she whispered to me:

'Magic puss cat.'

I purred and purred, and kissed her beautiful face. I patted the gold bead in the side of her nose. I searched those green, green eyes, past the brightness, and saw that the deep pain of losing Rocky was still there. It would be there for ever. But I was here now, and I was going to love her.

'Well ... I'm speechless,' said Penny.

TammyLee gazed and gazed at me, and a smudgy-looking tear rolled down her face. I licked it from her cheek, which was like a pale piece of velvet.

'It is you,' she whispered to me. 'I knew when I saw your photo in the paper. I knew it was you. Magic puss cat.'

I snuggled down in her arms and stretched my chin over her neck so that she could feel my purr vibrating through her. I wrapped my paw round the other side of her neck, hugging her like a human. She started smiling, and two dimples appeared in her cheeks.

'I'm speechless. Speechless,' said Penny again.

'Thank God for that,' said TammyLee wickedly, and the two women smiled at each other.

'Her name is Tallulah,' said Penny.

'Tallulah! That's lovely. It's like a song. Tallulah. I'll sing it to you one day, magic puss cat.'

I cuddled deeper into TammyLee's neck and throat, feeling as if I'd come home. I looked at Penny, and sent her a strong message. She got it.

'Well, it looks as if Tallulah knows you. She's certainly loving you,' said Penny.

'We do know each other. She used to run along the wall with me, in the moonlight, when...' The sadness in TammyLee's eyes rose to the surface, the deep ache of the mother love, like my mother's last look at me when we were ripped away from her. A forever pain.

'Please, please don't let anyone else have her,' pleaded TammyLee, suddenly vulnerable now, not arguing, not being bolshy, just appealing to Penny. 'Only I was going to take her home today.'

TammyLee sent me a picture of a lovely home with a fire, and a wide back door that opened into a sunny room made of glass. Beyond the glass was a back garden with a weeping willow and a view of the mountains. It was perfect. But Penny was looking serious and shaking her head.

'I'm sorry, my luvvy, but I can't let you take her.'

There was a silence. I clung tighter and purred harder round TammyLee's neck. I watched her aura turning to cracked glass, the way it had been that night. Grief and anxiety manifesting as anger. The anger flared through her like a bonfire, and I saw her looking at the gate. I saw she was thinking of making a run for it, with me in her arms.

'I know how much you want her,' said Penny kindly. 'You can wait a couple of days, can't you? Isn't Tallulah worth waiting for?'

I patted TammyLee's face and made her smile again as she fought against the anger.

'I can come tomorrow and look at your home,' Penny offered. 'And if it's OK, then I'll bring Tallulah to you in my car. She'll be safe, and I'd like to see her settled in. And I'm sure you'd like to know more about her, wouldn't you? She had a very nasty experience before she came here and you need to know about that, and know what to do if she shows any symptoms.'

A rush of sympathy changed TammyLee's defensive stance into softness and vulnerability. I sighed with relief as she said, 'OK then, if that's what it takes. So – can I really, really have her?'

'I hope so, my luvvy,' said Penny warmly. 'I do hope so.'

TammyLee put me down reluctantly and I wove myself around her legs as she and Penny went out through the two gates.

'Bye for now, Tallulah.' TammyLee looked down into my face. 'Don't look so anxious.

95

I'll see you soon, magic puss cat.'

I bounded up to the highest perch and saw her walking away down the farm track, getting smaller and smaller. She turned once to blow me a kiss and her bangles flashed in the sun. I watched her get on the bus that came grinding up the hill every day, and I followed it with my eyes so that I would know which direction to take to find her, if I had to. The bus turned right, away from the mountains, and headed along the road beside the river, the road that led into the town where I had lived with Gretel.

I ran round and round the pen, meowing, searching for an escape route. And again, I was distraught. TammyLee had come to find me, and Penny wouldn't let her take me!

Learning to wait, learning to trust, was a hard lesson for me. The pen seemed to be getting smaller, and my panic was like a whirlwind, engulfing me. When it reached an unbearable intensity, I noticed the black tom-cat sitting close to his fence, watching me in concern. He meowed and reached out a paw to me. We touched noses through the fence, and it was the first time I'd communicated with him. I'd dismissed him as a boring, fat, switched-off cat.

I sat still for a moment, to see if he would

communicate, and he did, telepathically. First, he leaned his solid black body against the fence, so that I could feel his warmth, and encouraged me with little purr-meows in his throat. We pressed against each other through the wire, and I sensed the words he was sending me.

'Be still,' he was telling me. 'Be still and listen.'

Hearing and listening are different things for a cat. Hearing is physical – hearing the wind in the trees, the traffic, the footsteps, the creak of doors. Listening is going inside a balloon of silence, sitting perfectly still and waiting.

The black cat joined me in this, and I felt his serenity and his wisdom. Why hadn't I done this before? All I'd done in that pen was sleep, play and panic, sleep, play and panic. In the black cat's benevolent presence, I was aware of him staring at my aura. What was he looking at?

Colours. He was showing me colours that flickered through my aura like those of a dragonfly in the sun. He was staring at a light in the air above and around me. He was showing me my angel!

'Wow,' I thought. 'It's been so long.' It seemed a lifetime ago when I was 'Fuzzball', that I'd talked with my angel. Well, I didn't talk; I listened, soaking up her words like the soothing heat of the sun.

'Tallulah,' she said, and it sounded like a song. 'Tallulah! All is well. You will go to TammyLee on the right day, when the sun is a deep gold. But first, you must wait, and trust. We have set this up for you so that you can begin your true work as Tallulah – a strong, wise and loving cat. The work will take many years, for TammyLee is a beautiful soul caught in a difficult life. She and her family will need you.'

'I wish I had a friend,' I said, 'like this black cat, or like the dog, Harriet, who rescued me when I was tiny. I've never had a friend, only a human. I've been lonely.'

'You will have a friend: Amber. Wait and see. Amber is waiting for you, and she is lonely too.'

'Who is she?' I asked, but my angel wouldn't tell me. She wanted to say something else.

'I've tried so often to talk to you, Tallulah,' she said. 'And you've always been too busy. Your life will spiral out of control if you don't practice stillness regularly.'

I agreed that I would and, as the colours of my angel muted into the night, I slept, right there against the wire, with the black cat still pressed against me on his side of the fence.

The sun was golden as Penny drove me past the fields of sheep, along the babbling river towards the town. I sat up smartly in the cat cage, noticing everything, my whiskers quivering with excitement.

'Here we are, Tallulah – your new home.' Penny swung the car away from the big roundabout, down a leafy lane and into a driveway. As soon as the tyres crunched over the gravel, I heard a dog barking deep inside the house. And I could hear another sound – the burble of water rushing over stones. The river was very close.

TammyLee came running across the lawn. I meowed as she reached the car, breathless, and full to the brim of love for me. I kissed her bangled arm through the wire mesh.

'Don't let her out yet,' warned Penny as she took my cage out of the car. The air smelled of sweet apples, and sheep and the briny river. After my time in the pen, I so needed to be on the grass and in the trees.

'I'll bring her in.' Penny seemed reluctant to let go of me. 'I want to see her reaction to Amber. And there's some papers to sign.'

She carried me into this awesome house,

which smelled of roast chicken and oranges, and, yes, it smelled of damp dog as well. The barking started again, a man's voice yelled, 'QUIET,' and it stopped.

'Here she is,' said TammyLee. 'This is Tallulah. Isn't she a darling?'

A man and a woman were looking into the cage at me, and I immediately observed that the woman was ill. Her aura was bright but fragile, and she sat in a wheelchair.

'This is Mum,' said TammyLee, and I did my best to smile there in the cage, giving a little purr-meow and dancing my eyes at the poor sick woman with the sweet face. 'Her name is Diana.'

Penny unfastened the cage door. I paused, fluffed my fur, and swanned out, looking round at everyone with my golden eyes full of joy. My family!

'And this is Dad.' TammyLee showed me the man, and he looked at me kindly under bushy eyebrows. He was obviously important, and powerful, his aura had an orange glow. I rubbed myself around his legs and felt him touch the tip of my fluffy tail.

'Hello, Tallulah,' he said, 'I'm Max,' and immediately I sensed he was holding something back, some secret he was bursting to tell me.

'Shall we do it?' he asked eagerly. 'Shall we introduce them?'

'No time like the present,' said Diana in a thin squeak of a voice.

'Best get it over with,' said Penny.

Max got up and opened a glass door into the conservatory. 'Now you be a good girl, Amber. Don't you dare even THINK about barking.'

I stared in utter joy. A dog! My own dog! And what a beauty. Amber was golden, silky and magnificent. She stood in the doorway with the light shining through the silver plume of her wagging tail. Her eyes were anxious and she went stiff when she saw me there with my tail up. I ran straight to her and kissed her on the nose.

'Oh, my goodness!' cried Penny.

Amber looked down at me like a goddess. Then she lay on her belly and sniffed at me, and whimpered.

'It's all right, Amber,' said TammyLee. 'Tallulah wants to be friends with you.'

Amber turned her head away from my kisses. She shivered all over and started creeping along the floor towards TammyLee.

'You great big coward.' Max laughed at Amber, loudly, and the dog looked hurt.

'Don't laugh at her. Poor Amber,' said

TammyLee, 'she's frightened of doing something wrong.'

I was impressed with her intuition. Amber seemed terribly uncomfortable with me rubbing against her throat and kissing her. She lifted a paw and put it on my back, and when I twisted out from under it, she jumped back as if she expected me to scratch her.

'They'll be fine,' said Penny. 'Tallulah's so laid-back.'

But I was disappointed. I'd fallen instantly in love with Amber and I felt rebuffed. I jumped up into TammyLee's arms for a cuddle, and she carried me slowly round the room, whispering to me, telling me what everything was. She carried me into the conservatory and showed me the garden, and Amber's bed. Amber followed us, her tail down, her eyes worried. She got on to her beanbag bed and stamped it round and around with a loud crunching noise, then slumped down on it and lay staring at the floor.

I needed time alone with Amber, and it didn't happen until early the next morning. I'd slept in three places: first, in the cat bed, ten minutes, then I tried all the chairs and found a little old one with a saggy seat, which was perfect. Two hours later, I got up, stretched, and explored every corner of the downstairs, up over the bookshelves first. I even took out a book with my paw and opened it, thought about shredding it, but there was too much else to inspect: over the mantelpiece, up the thick curtains and along the shelf at the top, where I found a spider to play with; under the massive sofa, where I practised being a flat cat. A lot of stuff was under there: slippers, a soggy tennis ball, a revolting old bone, a plastic rabbit, a tweed cap that smelled like a car. Obviously, these were Amber's treasures, and she was too big to get them out. Respectfully, I reversed out and went to the closed door of the conservatory, to look at Amber through the glass. Curled up in a ball on her bed, she was having a nightmare. Her paws were twitching and she was making squeaky little woofs in her throat.

I felt lonely and wanted to be with her, but she didn't like me. Upset and alone in the strange house, I crept through the hall and sniffed the night through a crack in the front door. I yearned to go out and taste the summer night, lie on the cool soft grass and watch the stars above me. My entire life had been doors and cages. I looked at the stairs, wanting to communicate with TammyLee.

She had to understand my need for freedom.

So I ended up slinking upstairs and into her bedroom. It smelled like flowers, and there were piles of glittery clothes and beads and hard shoes everywhere. A line of teddy bears patrolled the shelf above the bed, and I'd never really seen teddy bears before. They weren't asleep, and their glass eyes spooked me so much that I wailed in fright.

'Come on, darling, magic puss cat.' TammyLee was awake instantly and patting the bed quilt. I'd never been allowed on Gretel's bed, so I hesitated.

'Come on, Tallulah. It's OK. You've got me now.' She reached down and scooped me into the softest pillowy place I'd ever experienced. It smelled of pansies, and felt softer than the deepest grasses. I sank my paws into it, dough punching and purring, and went to sleep, a happy cat, with TammyLee's hand on my fur.

TammyLee was fast asleep when I heard the dawn outside. Pigeons were cooing and jackdaws chack-chacking. I jumped onto the windowsill and sat in the pink sunlight, watching the swallows, tiny and fast, zooming in wide arcs through the sky, and their high pitched voices sounded free and joyful. I wanted to be out there, prowling on the lawns, exploring, climbing the fence and inspecting the garden next door. I wanted to feel the earth under my paws, and taste the grass, and hear the bees waking up as the sun rose.

The smell of toast and bacon wafted up the stairs, so I padded down with my tail up and found TammyLee's dad at the table in the kitchen with Amber leaning against his legs. She turned when she saw me, but only her ears moved, and the very tip of her tail wagged. I longed to pounce on it and play, but it was too early to take liberties like that.

'Hello, Tallulah.' Max didn't move but kept his arm protectively around Amber, and his coffee mug in the other hand. I rubbed myself adoringly on Amber's creamy gold chest and she stuck her nose high in the air to avoid me.

'I must get off to work now.' Dad got up and took his plate to the sink, giving Amber a scrap of bacon rind, which she snapped and swallowed. Then he gave me some milk and wagged his finger at Amber. 'Don't you TOUCH it. That's the cat's breakfast. Leave it.'

I lapped it up quickly, while Amber sat watching me. Max headed for the door, a black case in his hand. 'No, Tallulah,' he said. 'You're not allowed out yet. You get to know Amber.' And his soap-scented hand pushed me back gently as I tried to go out.

Was I still a prisoner?

Miffed, I sat washing, and Amber must have sensed my sadness, for she crept towards me and touched me with a big soft paw. I deliberately continued washing. I could manage perfectly well without a dog who didn't like me, thank you.

Amber listened to the sound of Max's car rolling over the gravel, then leaving with a smart zippy sort of roar. The house was quiet, and I was alone with my beautiful goddess of a dog, and she didn't like me.

Once the car had gone, Amber relaxed. She started sending me messages, in the way that animals do, by telepathy. It's so much easier than trying to actually speak like humans do, and it changes so smoothly from images to words and back again.

The first message Amber sent me was that she loved Max, but he dominated her too much. She was a more confident dog when he wasn't there telling her what to do. She did want to be friends with me, but she'd never had a cat friend before, and she was nervous.

She gave me an experimental lick on the

top of my head, and I stopped being huffy and let her lick my back the way Harriet had done. When I'd had enough, I gave her a pat on the nose, being careful to keep my claws retracted. She lay down on her side, and let me cuddle up to her and she wanted me to purr right next to her ear. She lay there, thumping her tail, and I even dared to play with it.

Suddenly, Amber sat up and listened attentively, her nose twitching. It made my hackles rise and my tail bush out in the spooky silence, not knowing why she was listening. Something was going to happen. I heard a bleeping noise from upstairs. Then I was almost knocked over as Amber took off in a whirl of wispy fur. She skidded through the hall and thundered up the stairs, her tail wagging furiously. I heard a squeal from TammyLee's room, and Amber reappeared with her aura on fire, her ears flying and her mouth smiling. She charged down the stairs, grabbed a shoe from the mat, and did a wild circle with her back all bunched up. I leaped out of the way onto the back of the sofa with my bottle-brush tail kinked in the air.

I watched in disbelief as Amber lolloped upstairs again. I peered up there and saw her skid round the doorway into TammyLee's room. I heard the clonk as she dropped the shoe and loud laughter from TammyLee. The laughing seemed to add fire and speed to Amber's performance. She lolloped down again, did another mad circle, pausing to snatch the other shoe, before belting upstairs again like an earthquake. By the time she had done it about six times, my fur had gone flat again, and I understood this was a game she played. Every morning, she told me as she flashed past, every morning she heard TammyLee's alarm clock and galloped up the stairs. It started the day with peals of laughter, even the china in the kitchen was ringing with it.

It filled me with joy. Before long, I knew, I would join in the game, if I could keep out of the way of those flying paws. I'd hide under the stairs and leap out at Amber's tail as she soared past. Ah, I was going to have fun in this house!

I wondered if there would be a postman.

I waited until Amber ran downstairs for the final time, puffing and snorting, and too hot. She flopped down on the cold tiles in the kitchen, and I arranged my fur, put my tail up and walked upstairs nicely, to say good morning to TammyLee.

She was sitting in front of a mirror, fixing

her hair, dragging some of it back and some of it forward, then pulling out curly strands to hang round her face.

'Tallulah!' she breathed, and picked me up as if I was the most precious treasure. She put down the comb and the funny-looking strand of pink hair that she'd been trying to add to the hairstyle.

I sat on her lap and stared into her eyes, and what I saw there told me it was time for serious stuff. It wasn't the time to purr, or to play. It was time to listen.

TammyLee said some nice things to me first, the sort of blanket comments people offer to cats, like, 'Aren't you beautiful?' and 'You're SUCH a lovely cat.' Then it moved on to, 'I can't believe I found you again. I knew it was you, and I saw you on TV.'

I maintained my searching stare, and her voice dropped to a whisper. 'I don't deserve you. I'm a bad girl. And you know, don't you, Tallulah? You were there when I ... did what I did.'

I responded with a mini purr-meow, and sat still, watching and waiting.

'You know what I did ... that terrible night.' TammyLee was stroking me with her hands, one each side of me, her slim fingers buried in my fur. 'And you went back, didn't you?

109

You saw my baby – my Rocky. I think about him all the time.'

I licked the tears from her cheeks, but more and more came and she moved her hands to press hard against her temples. I watched the deep, dark pain rise to the surface, and sink back again into the green depths of her eyes.

'I knew I was pregnant, and I didn't dare tell Dad – he'd have killed me – and I had mum to look after, and my school stuff. I kept hoping I'd miscarry, and I hid my bump under loose clothes, 'cause I'm fat anyway. I told people I was bingeing on cream cakes and stuff. Oh, you're a gorgeous cat, Tallulah...' she paused to give me an extra cuddle, and gazed into my attentive eyes. 'Even when he started moving, I kind of convinced myself it wasn't true – I was in TOTAL denial, and so, so scared. I went into labour on the way to school and I was terrified, Tallulah – I ran away and sat in the churchyard. I thought about topping myself. I stayed there all day, until it got bad – really bad. I went in the toilets and he was born so quickly,' her voice dropped to a whisper – 'and the placenta came out too – it was terrible. Thank God no one was in there, 'cause I was screaming and so was he. I thought I was gonna die. Then I cut the cord with nail scissors – it took ages – and all I had to wrap him in was a scarf ... and he ... he looked at me, and I can't get his little face out of my mind. I panicked then, didn't think about anything except how I could get rid of him. I'm so wicked, Tallulah. I'm evil. I'll never forgive myself ... and I can't tell anyone, only you.'

I listened and listened, and for the first time in my life, I felt needed. I was aware of an angel who was holding TammyLee in her shining arms.

'I was fourteen,' she whispered. 'I was desperate ... and I'm still desperate, Tallulah ... I'm a prisoner, you see. Like you were, in that pen. I'm a prisoner.'

She rocked herself to and fro, her aura flooded with the memories. I tasted the intensity of her secret pain. But I was puzzled. Why was she a prisoner? And did that mean I would be one too? I put my paws around her neck and hugged her, purring a loud vibrational purr. That pain inside her needed to come out and, over time, I would coax it out with my purring, healing love. She hugged me back, and rocked me, and whispered, 'You're a wonderful, fantabulous, gorgeous cat.'

I chose that moment to send her a strong message, that I wanted to go outside. She didn't get it, so I jumped on to the window-sill and meowed, looking down at the tantalising garden.

'Are you hungry?' asked TammyLee.

I looked at the garden again and back into her eyes.

'Oh, you want to go out? Of course you can, darling. Penny said to keep you in for a few days, but you're not going to run away, are you, Tallulah? I'll take you out after breakfast … but first…'

As she spoke, I heard Diana's thin voice calling out:

'I'm awake dear. Are you coming?'

'Yes, I'll be right there, Mum.'

TammyLee picked me up.

'You can come and watch,' she said. 'I look after Mum. I'm her carer. I've gotta do everything for her. Get her up, help her wash and dress, then I do the housework and stuff. Then I go to school, but not today, 'cause it's holiday, whatever that's supposed to mean!'

She sounded bitter and tired, but as she carried me down a corridor and into her mum's bedroom, everything changed, and, if I'd been a human, I'd have gasped in surprise.

The room she took me into was full of angels. One at each side of the bed head, and one on each side at the foot of the bed – they were still as water lilies, their colours lemon and white. They were so dazzling that I could hardly see their faces, or anything else in the room.

In that wonderful moment, I became my true soul self again, the Queen of Cats. I puffed out my fur, and my aura became huge, my eyes like bright suns as I sat soaking up the light from the angels, and purring so loudly that the vibration sent stardust whizzing through my aura. I looked round at each angel in turn, and realised that these were 'comfort angels'. I'd seen many of them in the spirit world, and they rarely moved, but just emanated love and stillness. Sometimes, they sent out tendrils of healing colour, and I noticed they were doing this to TammyLee as she stood by the bed. They were wrapping her in ribbons of love.

Then it hit me.

TammyLee couldn't see the angels.

She couldn't feel the waves of light from their love. She was earthbound.

'What a funny cat.' TammyLee's mum was saying. 'Why is she sitting with her back to me ... and what is she looking at?'

I turned round and saw Diana sitting up in bed, her cheeks hollow, her eyes dancing, her white hands stretching out to stroke me. I loved her straightaway.

'I'm Diana,' she said, 'but you can call me Mum.'

She was a beautiful soul, and I decided to call her Diana, not Mum. I walked up to the bed and made a fuss of her, kissing her thin face.

I settled down in the corner of the bed under one of the angels, and watched TammyLee in surprise. When she was helping Diana, she seemed like a different person from the crying, desperate girl I'd seen. She acted like a cat lady, being calm and cheerful, doing everything, even the awkward jobs, with kindness and skill, her bangles jangling as she washed and dressed Diana. The two women talked happily, mostly about me and Amber and the garden. It was obvious to me that TammyLee loved her mum very much. I felt a twinge of envy. If only I'd had my mum, Jessica, in my life, I might have been a better cat.

TammyLee helped Diana to walk with a frame, to the top of the stairs, and sat her in a chair. She flicked a switch and the chair glided down the stairs to Amber, who was waiting at the bottom, her tail wagging, her front paws quivering with excitement.

We all had breakfast together, and Tammy-Lee did everything, hardly sitting down herself, but marching about with toast in her hand.

'Hasn't Tallulah settled down well?' remarked Diana. 'What a GOOD cat!'

I glowed. After the names Gretel had called me, hearing that was like a healing touch on my soul.

Chapter Seven

SOLOMON

The room with the angels soon became one of my favourite places to curl up during the day when TammyLee had gone to school. I loved the softness and the colours of Diana's room, the wind chimes tinkling in the open window, the wide windowsill with velvet cushions, the way the sun streamed in and gilded the sparkly scarves hanging on the back of the door. A glass crystal in the window splashed rainbows over everything, and once, for a magic moment, I had one on my fur. I lay very still, squinting at the intense colour as it rose and fell with my breathing, feeling it healing something deep within me, a part of me that had been damaged by the time in Gretel's hot car.

Amber acted strangely in Diana's room. She wouldn't stand up and wag her tail. She'd hover in the doorway and then creep in on her belly to see Diana, and sit with her chin on the bed and just the tip of her tail flipping as she offered Diana first one paw, then the other. From my lofty perch on top of the bookshelves, I studied her weird behaviour and the way she and Diana gazed at each other. If Diana closed her eyes, Amber would whine and push her nose into the limp hand hanging over the side of the bed.

'It's all right, Amber. I'm not going to snuff it yet,' she said, opening her eyes, and I watched the relief flood through the dog's soft face. Sadness, and intense anxiety, I thought – I have to get to know this dog, she's such a complex being.

Later, I lay on the doormat next to Amber's shining warm body.

'Why are you so sad around Diana?' I asked.

Amber gave a deep sigh and I could see

116

her processing the reply. I waited.

'Diana is ill, and I don't want her to die,' she said, and a tear rolled out of the corner of her left eye.

I made a fuss, purring and rubbing my head against her and she seemed to like it now. She left her head down for me, then rolled onto her side and let me walk all over her, stepping over her paws and along her back, and purring into her ear.

'I'm Diana's dog,' said Amber. 'She came and chose me when I was a puppy, and she taught me everything, even how to cross the road safely. She used to take me for lovely walks along the river and up into the hills, and she was never in a hurry like TammyLee and Max. She liked to sit for ages and listen to the water. She said it had a heartbeat.'

'I'd like to hear that,' I said. 'Next time you go to the river, I'm going to come.'

'You won't like it,' said Amber. 'We go through a park with big dogs racing about. It's no place for a cat, believe me.'

'I'll find a way,' I said, visualising myself on TammyLee's shoulder or running through the tree-tops like a squirrel.

'And there are lots of people,' Amber said, 'but, when I go with TammyLee, she takes me out of the park and up to the waterfalls and it's quiet. We go to a pool and she likes to swim with me.'

'Swim?' I was horrified. 'I shan't be doing THAT.'

TammyLee tried to discourage me from going on her walks with Amber, but I passionately wanted to go. So I learned to anticipate when it was going to happen, and slipped outside to hide in the garden, then belt after them with my tail flying.

The first few times, TammyLee tried to take me home, but I wouldn't let her catch me, and, eventually, she understood my need to go with them, and realised I was well able to look after myself. Avoiding the park, she headed down a footpath, which led straight to the river, close enough to home for me to go on my own! I couldn't wait to do some private hunting.

We had a wonderful summer, and when the chill of autumn came and the river glowed with floating leaves, TammyLee dragged lots of wood logs inside and lit a cosy fire. Amber and I sat watching the flames and warming ourselves, while TammyLee marched around, cooking, cleaning and caring.

'She's a real angel,' Diana said as I dozed on her lap. 'I'm so lucky to have such a kind daughter. I wish Max wasn't so hard on her.

But we love her, don't we, Tallulah?'

I looked at Diana's expectant eyes and wondered if she knew about Rocky. No, my angel said. But I wished TammyLee would tell her. Diana was her mum. She should know her daughter cried every single night before she went to sleep, and the tears were tears of regret and longing for her lost child.

'I would have loved him, Tallulah,' she wept to me. 'I do love him, but I'll never see him again, and when he grows up, he'll never forgive me. How would you feel if your mum dumped you?'

I knew the pain of abandonment, but I couldn't tell her how bad I'd felt when Joe dumped us in the hedge, and again when Gretel threw me out for wrecking the Christmas tree.

I worried about Christmas. When was it? Would there be a tree that I mustn't play with? I asked Amber.

'It's soon,' she said. 'I know it's in the winter when the nights are dark. Max takes me out in the night and the frost burns my paws. He leans on the railings and looks at the stars, and I'm not allowed in the water. And sometimes he walks me into the town and we admire the coloured lights on people's homes.'

That gave me a clue. As the nights got

longer, the afternoons gloomier, I noticed coloured lights appearing on the houses and in the trees. I worried and worried, and when I heard a rustling noise and saw Max dragging a Christmas tree through the door, I panicked.

I was on the hearth rug with Amber, nice and warm in front of a blazing fire, and I was in the middle of washing. When I saw the Christmas tree, my eyes must have turned huge and black, for TammyLee said, 'What's the matter, Tallulah? Tallulah! Don't run away!'

I didn't wait for her to catch me. I bolted, like a squirrel crossing the road, into the kitchen, past my supper, which I hadn't yet eaten, and charged through the cat flap, up the frosty garden and into the road. Without stopping to think, I sped down the footpath towards the river.

When my paws started to burn from the frost, I thought about Amber. I had to find a hiding place where she wouldn't find me, because I wasn't going back. No, I'd hide out there for the winter, until that Christmas tree had gone, and then I'd creep back. It wasn't going to be easy, but I had a thick luxurious coat to keep me warm.

My angel's voice whispered in my mind:

'Don't do this, Tallulah.' But I ignored her, and ran on, following the river upstream, until I reached the stone bridge where TammyLee had often taken me. I hoped the stones would be warm from the sun, but they were colder than ice. The whole earth ached with the chill of winter; down in the roots of grasses, the frost crackled and puddles creaked with ice.

Nearby was a good place to catch mice, a bank of mossy tree roots with numerous holes. Usually, it was easy. I only had to wait, watch and pounce. On this bitter night, not a single mouse appeared. The birds were silent. The air was still, and my breath was making tiny puffs of steam in the moonlight. I sat down to watch for mice, but found myself hypnotised by the enormous silver-gold moon, which was rising over the mountains, its light glinting on the flowing river and glazing the frosted stones of the old bridge. The moss and the bare twigs were coated with ice, and nothing moved. I felt like the only living creature out there, and yet ... something was watching me, making my fur stiff with fright. A fox? A prowling dog? Or some other strange creature of the night?

I listened for its footsteps.

The murmur of the water, the metallic

tinkling of frosted reeds and the cracking of ice along the riverbank. My whiskers glistened, my fur puffed out like a halo, and the tips of it had a haze of hoar frost. I seemed like a cat frozen in time, locked in a cocoon of magic moonlight, where something, some presence, was waiting for me.

I looked up at the bridge, and there he was, high on the top. A cat! My whiskers stiffened, my tail twitched in alarm. Was he real? He didn't look real. Even though his eyes shone green in the moonlight, he looked transparent, like a ghost cat. His presence was magnetic. I found myself creeping towards him, wanting his warmth and his company, yet knowing that wasn't what he could give me. He was a phantom, unmoving, but staring at me with calm intelligence.

I padded closer, my heart racing, and sat down at a respectful distance. Still the cat didn't move. I observed the curve of his whiskers, and the faint iridescence that came from his fur. It was blacker than the night, but he had a white chest and paws.

Something shifted in my memory. A time of being a baby kitten, under a bed, and this same cat had been there, watching me proudly, protectively.

My dad. Solomon!

Overwhelmed, I kept still and waited for him to speak. I wanted to run to him and touch noses, but something held me back, some invisible force between me and him.

'Tallulah!' he said at last, and a feeling of relief settled over me. 'I'm not a spirit cat, and I'm not really here. I'm with you in my thoughts, and I know you're in trouble. You must go home.'

'I can't,' I said.

'You can, and you must. You are too precious to live wild in the winter. It's your mission to be with TammyLee. She is calling you now. Listen!'

I did, and through the silvery night came the distant voice: 'Tallulah. Tallooolah!'

'It will be all right,' said Solomon. 'You can play and be joyful, and no one there will make you afraid. Take back your trust and your joy, and go home to the people you love.'

I cried to him, in gratitude. Even my angel hadn't found the right words like he had done.

Then I heard his purr, and it was louder than mine. It filled the echoing shell of winter. I gazed at Solomon and then he was gone, leaving only the purr in my heart. I turned and trotted homewards along the river, with the words ringing in my mind: 'Take back your trust and your joy.' He was right. Who had taken those treasures of the soul away from me? Gretel! I'd forgiven her, but I hadn't taken back my right to play and be joyful.

I paused, to look back at the bridge. It was dark against the moonlit river, and the mysterious cat had vanished. He'd left me a picture of where he really was on this winter night, curled up on the lap of a beautiful woman with long blonde hair who sat by a bright warm stove, stroking him and dreaming.

Solomon. I'd seen Solomon. My dad. My homeward trot quickened to a gallop, the mad dash of an ecstatic cat. I streaked along the riverbank, skidded round the corner and into the footpath, where I saw a torch shining at me and heard TammyLee's cry of joy as I ran to her with my tail up.

She carried me home, her cold cheek pressed against my fur. Through the gate, up the path and into the warm kitchen. My supper was still there, untouched.

'You wait till you see our Christmas tree,' she said, and I followed her into the lounge. I sat down next to Amber and gazed at the sparkling tree. I made up my mind not to touch it, only lie on my back under its branches and watch the reflections in the baubles. I was glad to be home.

Winter passed and it was spring again, and by then I was a confident and contented cat. I was even a bit fatter, which only added to my magnificence.

Every afternoon, Amber and I waited in the garden for TammyLee to come home from school. Amber's sensitivity was awesome, and she knew when the bus was coming, even if it was far away. She'd run to the gate, put her paws on top of it and bark, nearly knocking me over with her tail. I rearranged my ruffled fur and slipped under the gate, to run down the road and meet TammyLee. It always made her smile to see me welcoming her.

But one afternoon in May, it was different. Amber's tail went down and her ears drooped, as we waited. The bus came. We saw it trundle past the end of the road, and it didn't stop. Where was TammyLee?

I sat on the hot pavement, waiting, but she didn't come.

Something made me look up at the trees overhanging the next-door fence, and one was full of light. It swerved and danced, then settled into a familiar shape. My angel.

'Remember the tree, Tallulah,' she said, 'like this one.'

The perfume hit me. Elderflowers. My angel was showing me something important.

'It's an anniversary,' she explained. 'Humans count events in years, and when the time comes round again, they remember. The feelings return, stronger than before. Today is Rocky's first birthday, at the time when the elder tree flowers, as it will always be.'

Amber was whining behind the gate, and Diana was calling me from her window, but I hurried down the road. I knew exactly what I had to do. Follow the river. Go through the scary park with all the dogs, run beside the river towards the town, until I came to the elder tree where TammyLee had abandoned baby Rocky.

I'd wanted Amber to go with me, but instead, I found myself on a lone mission. The river shimmered in the heat, and a family of ducks were sleeping on the bank. When they saw me, they plopped into the water and swam across to the other side. It gave me an idea. Why not cross the river and be out of the reach of dogs, and people? I climbed the sturdy trunk of an oak tree and followed a curly branch with little ferns growing on it. Soon I was above the water, looking down at the swirls and the green of it flowing below me. The branch was getting thinner and thinner. I hesitated, then realised I couldn't turn round without falling into the river. Looking down at it made me dizzy

Frightened now, I clung to the thin branch, thinking about the logistics of turning round on it. A bunch of sheep stood on the opposite bank, looking at me, as if waiting for me to fall in. I meowed at them and they bleated back, and more sheep came skittering across the field to stare at me, a cat in a tree. I tuned in to their communal mind-set and found they were expecting me to jump. I thought about it. If I crept a bit further along the branch, I might risk a flying leap onto a green tuft of the bank that stuck out into the river. In a way, the hundred eyes of the sheep were encouraging me.

'Tallulah,' said my angel. 'Think about your name. Tallulah.'

From far away, Diana's clear bell-like voice was calling me from the window. 'Talloolah. Talloolah.' My name seemed to be woven into the whisper and burble of the water. The river's colours were the colours of my fur –

silver and black with tinges of gold. Roxanne had given me my name, and it meant 'Leaping water'.

As I hyped myself up for the jump, my name echoed up and down the river valley. Even a pigeon was cooing it from a tree, and a black bird, and angels from beyond the glistening edges of the world, all singing my name, inviting me to jump.

There was a moment of balance when I wobbled a little, and the branch dipped and creaked. A woman walking along the path gasped, 'Look at THAT CAT! It's not going to...'

I was a cat on fire. I took off in a spectacular swoosh of oak leaves, my back arched, my paws akimbo, my tail snaking. I held my breath. I was in the air and, in that moment, the sheep wheeled around and fled with a rumble of feet, and the woman screamed, 'It's going in the river!' Back in the garden, Amber was barking, and her barks were giving me energy.

Phew! I landed precisely on that green tuft with my heart racing, and Amber's barks changed to a howl as if she was saying good-bye. My angel turned up again, and she was laughing with joy, sending sparkles over the grass.

'Fuzzball could never have done that!' she said.

It was true. My name had power.

It seemed a good time to wash, so I started on my paws, which felt gritty. It's a privilege to be a cat. We don't gallop about, knocking things over like dogs. We stop to contemplate and take time to enjoy life.

While I was picking bits of moss from between my pads, I kept an eye on the sheep, who were now standing in a circle, looking at me with their hundred eyes. I wanted to touch noses with a sheep, so I pretended not to notice them as they tiptoed closer, blowing hot breath out of their nostrils. When they were right up close, I stretched elegantly, and walked towards them with my tail up. A shiver rippled through the flock. They hesitated while the ring-leader came forward and reached out to me with her velvety face. There was a glint in her yellowy eyes as we touched noses, and some of her steam got onto my whiskers. I sent her a quick message: 'If ever I'm lost, I might need you to keep me warm at night.'

She might have said, 'Yes,' but the moment of contact was brief. Obviously, she was spooked by me, and her courage ran out. She sprang back, and that fired up the rest of the sheep. They took off again, some of them leaping in the air, and fled to the far corner of the field, where they turned and stared back at me with their hundred eyes.

Mildly annoyed, I finished washing my paws and set off along the springy turf of the riverbank, towards the town. Through the next field, and the next, through tall grasses and flowers so rich with pollen that it made me sneeze. It was hard for me to remember where I was going, and not get distracted by the new places I was discovering; places where tantalising butterflies flitted and bees hummed. There would be voles and mice hidden in that grass. I put it on my 'places to go' list, for when I could slip away and do some private hunting.

My angel was ahead of me, glistening like a dragonfly, leading me on an ever more challenging path, through back gardens that sloped down to the river, over fences and compost heaps, through tangles of honeysuckle and briars. At last, I came to a road between the gardens and the river. There were wheelie bins, boxes of cardboard and empty tins that smelled of cat food. More temptation.

A perfectly good piece of cheese was lying on the gravel next to one bin. I picked it up gingerly and dived under some bushes to enjoy it in private. The cheese was chewy but deliciously salty and it took me a while to eat it. My mind was on TammyLee, imagining her sitting under that elder tree by herself, remembering Rocky and breaking her heart. I should be there.

Even as I had that thought, I heard the clonk of shoes on the other side of the river and there was TammyLee, trudging towards home, her school bag slung over one shoulder, her head down, her cheeks red from crying. I was too late. Gretel's words rang in my mind: 'You BAD CAT.' I'd got distracted by the sheep and the piece of cheese. What a disgrace after doing that magnificent jump.

And how was I going to get back across the river?

I meowed at TammyLee but she didn't hear me. She had those little black earphones in her ears, listening to music. I started back the way I had come, wanting to go with her, but then a worse thought came to me. Even if I did go back along the bank and through the sheep field, I couldn't possibly jump up onto that branch. I sat down to think, and my angel came again, hovering over the water.

'You must go on, to the foot bridge,' she said. 'I've told you, there are no bad cats,

Tallulah. You must cross the bridge and go to the elder tree, then you will know why. Go quickly now. Quickly.'

She whisked me along under the shimmering umbrella of her wings, and I felt protected. No one stopped me. No dogs barked at me. I reached the foot bridge and trotted over it, relieved to be back on my side of the river.

I looked for the elder tree, and it had gone. My fur began to prickle and I crouched down in the long grass to see what had changed. The tree, and the old wall, had been removed, and in its place was a new-looking patio with slabs of dark grey and gold, and in the middle was a bench of polished red wood. A new tree had been planted next to it and it wasn't an elder. This one had thick clusters of pink flowers.

It felt strangely disappointing. I'd been looking forward to some magic time with TammyLee under that special elder tree. So why had my angel brought me here, hustling me along the riverbank, only to see a bench?

I watched and waited.

I could hear the river, and the traffic in the town. Then voices and footsteps. I sat up to see who was coming along the path and it was two women with pushchairs, one behind the other, talking in low voices that seemed to belong to the sleepy afternoon.

They stood looking at the bench, running their fingers over the polished wood, and touching the square of brass that reflected the sun. I could tell there were babies in the two pushchairs, even though they had their back to me, each had an angel of light like two splashes of gold in the air, not huge but intense and comforting. It made me purr as I lay hidden in the grass, watching. Since that night with Rocky, I loved babies and wanted to be close to them whenever I had the chance.

'Wait, Tallulah,' said my angel. 'The right moment will come, if you listen.'

I listened, and there were grasshoppers zeet-zeeting in the hot grass, and pigeons coo-cooing, and the distant thump-thump of music from the town. My angel pointed at the two women with a finger that sliced through the air like a blade of turquoise light. So I focused on their faces and their conversation. I knew their names – Maddie and Kaye – and Kaye was doing most of the talking.

'Wasn't it a lovely thing to do?' she was saying. 'To put a bench here. And such a posh one. Must have cost a fortune.'

'Lovely,' agreed Maddie.

'Linda paid for it,' said Kaye, 'and she wouldn't have her name on it. She's like that.'

The name Linda tweaked my memory of the kind lady who had found Rocky and cried over him. The lady with the comfortable shoulders and the shivering dog.

Both women turned and looked at the square of brass again and were silent for a moment. I wondered what was on it. Pity I couldn't read. I was getting twitchy, wanting to go out there with my tail up, and wanting to go home to TammyLee. Had she been here? Had she cried on this special day, and needed me to be with her, while I was messing about instead of coming here?

'You're getting negative again. Just listen,' said my angel.

'But what am I doing here?' I asked.

'Wait,' she repeated patiently, 'and soon you will know.'

One of the babies was waking up. I could see a plump little hand waving from the pushchair.

'She's too hot. Aren't you, my darling?' Maddie stood up, lifted the baby girl out and sat down again, nursing her.

Then the other baby started to scream and

134

kick vigorously at the pushchair. Kaye was on her feet instantly.

'What's the matter, darling? Want to get out, do you? All right, all right. Wait a minute while Mummy undoes the straps.'

'He's a bruiser!' said Maddie, laughing, and the baby cried even more furiously while Kaye struggled to lift him out. He was big and energetic, his face red with the crying, his arms and legs thrashing.

'Here we go,' said Kaye, heaving him onto her lap. 'He's in a strop.'

'Go out there,' said my angel, 'and purr.'

I pulled up my tail, straightened my whiskers, and walked out into the sunshine.

'Oh, look, a cat. A pretty pussycat,' said Kaye. The effect on the crying child was instant.

'Tat!' he shouted, and clapped his fat little hands. 'Tat!'

I jumped up onto the warm bench between the two women and turned on the purring, rubbing my head against first one and then the other.

'Oh, lovely … friendly cat. You stroke him, he's soft,' said Maddie, putting her baby girl's tiny hand on my fur. It felt like a butterfly.

'Tat!' The baby boy was getting more and more excited. 'Mine.'

'No, he's not your cat,' said Kaye. 'But you can stroke him ... or her, is it?'

'Tat ... mine,' insisted the baby boy, and he held out his arms to me. I went to him, purring, and let him put both his chubby arms around my neck.

'Don't strangle the poor cat,' said Kaye, laughing.

I let the baby boy love me and listen to my purr. I kissed his red nose and he giggled, patting me a bit too hard. I sat up and looked at him. I saw turquoise eyes, full of astonishment. I saw a mole on his cheek. And I knew why my angel had brought me here.

It was Rocky.

Chapter Eight

ROCKY

I stared into Rocky's soul and he stared back. Going deep into those turquoise eyes, I saw that Rocky was ages old and full of light. I kept staring deeper and deeper until I discovered a pocket of darkness, which I recognised instantly as the pain of abandonment. Once I'd found it, I wanted to heal it, so I purred and purred, and stretched my paws over his steady little heart.

'You can't,' said my angel. 'It is part of him, part of his journey. He will always carry that memory, as you carry yours.'

I kept purring, sending stars into Rocky's soul with all my energy, thinking I might never see him again, but knowing I had to find a way to reunite him with his true mother. I sent him pictures from my mind, of TammyLee, and how bitterly she regretted dumping him, how much she loved him. He accepted them, but his eyes looked puzzled. He pointed at Kaye.

'Mum ... mum,' he said, and looked back at me 'Tat! Mine.'

I kissed Rocky on the nose and he squealed with delight.

'You shouldn't let cats kiss babies,' said Maddie, disapprovingly.

Kaye smiled. 'I don't believe that. It's medical paranoia.'

'But what about germs?' Maddie was holding her own baby very tightly.

'What about them? We can't let germs stand in the way of LOVE,' said Kaye passionately. 'This cat is giving him so much love. Look at her ... purring like a sewing machine.' She put her hand on my back. 'I can feel the vibration right through her body. And Rocky's loving it. Aren't you, darling?'

'Tat!' shouted Rocky. Then he reached out and patted the square brass in the middle of the bench. 'Dat?' he asked.

'That's a commemorative plaque, sweetheart,' said Kaye. 'And it says "ROCKY'S BENCH".'

There was a silence while the words sank into our minds.

'Are you going to tell him about it?' asked Maddie.

'Not yet,' Kaye replied, kissing Rocky's silky dark head. 'When he's old enough. And IF Social Services decide we can actually adopt him. We want to so much. He's my LIFE, aren't you, Rocky?'

I turned my attention to Kaye, and gave her an intense stare.

'This cat's got such amazing eyes,' she said. 'Golden and so knowing.'

'Wasn't a cat there when Rocky was found?' asked Maddie. 'You showed me a press cutting. It did look like this one. Didn't the police think it might belong to the mother?'

'They did, but it belonged to an old lady on the other side of town,' said Kaye, but the joy in her eyes had clouded and I saw that she was afraid of losing Rocky. She looked away, and I felt our contact had been abruptly shut down.

'We'd better get back, Maddie. I've got to start Greg's tea.'

'Dad, Dad!' shouted Rocky.

'Yes ... Daddy's tea. And Rocky's tea and a birthday cake with one candle.' She stood up and gently lifted Rocky away from me. 'Say goodbye to the lovely puss cat.'

Rocky struggled and screamed. 'Tat ... mine.' Kaye rolled her eyes and wrestled him into the pushchair. He kicked and stomped, shaking the whole pushchair, while Maddie was putting her quiet little baby into hers.

'Come on,' Kaye said, over the screaming. 'The sooner we go, the sooner he'll calm down. Calm down, Rocky, it's not your cat. We can see her another day.'

Maddie wagged a finger at me. 'Don't you follow us!'

I sat down on the warm bench and watched them go, Kaye walking briskly with her thrashing cargo. His screams faded into the distance. 'Tat ... mine. Tat ... mine.'

I decided to stay out, and make my way home after dark, thinking that most dogs would have gone home and it would be safe for me to run through the park. Rocky's bench was perfect for me to sleep on. But first, I checked it out for any sign that TammyLee had been there. Right in the middle, near the brass plaque, I detected a faint scent of her. Then between the slats of wood, I saw something interesting.

I jumped down to investigate, and, hidden behind one of the bench legs, was a small posy of flowers, wild flowers mostly, but in the centre was a single red rose, tied together with one of the glittery rubber bands TammyLee used in her hair. Her scent was on it, and I knew for sure that she had been there and left a posy for Rocky.

It was dark when I arrived home, and TammyLee was in the garden with a torch, looking for me. My tail was bushed out and the fur along my spine was stiff with fright after my long trip home alone in the dark.

'Oh, there you are!' cried TammyLee. 'Where have you BEEN?'

I jumped straight into her arms, and she felt me all over. 'Are you OK, Tallulah? Look at your tail! It's like a hairbrush. What scared you?'

If only I could talk her language and tell her I'd seen Rocky. All I could do was purr and reach up to her concerned face with my paws. She'd been crying. Sobs lingered, deep down in her chest, spasmodically surfacing. I sensed the pain.

'Dad's mad with me,' she said as she carried me indoors. 'For walking home along the river on my own, and being late, and being rude.'

There was a tense atmosphere in the house, as if something was going to explode. Max was hunched at the table, frowning at his laptop. He glanced up with cold eyes.

'Thank God for that,' he said. 'Where was she?'

'She just appeared,' said TammyLee, 'like cats do.'

'Now perhaps we'll get some PEACE,' said Max wearily.

TammyLee stood there with me in her arms. I nuzzled against her and the pulse throbbing in her neck felt hot.

'Is that all you care about, Dad?' she asked. 'So-called "peace".'

Max pursed his lips and narrowed his eyes. 'Dad?'

'I am not going to engage with further provocation,' said Max, and a hard grey shell closed around his aura. He turned back to his laptop and tapped at the keys like a terrier digging a hole.

'Fine. Don't bother,' said TammyLee. She put me down and marched into the kitchen. I ran to see Amber, who was lying quietly on her bed, her ears drooping and only the tip of her tail moving. She whined and lifted a paw to me. I wanted to describe my adventure by the river, and tell her about Rocky's turquoise eyes, but she wasn't in a receptive mood.

'There was a terrible row,' she told me. 'TammyLee was in a temper and she burned Max's tea and slammed the plate down on the table. She shouted and swore at him, and every time Max tried to say something, she shouted even louder. I hated it, I hid behind the curtain, and now I've been on my bed for too long and I haven't had a walk.'

Amber looked miserable and anxious. I gave her lots of love, weaving my way round her, brushing her face with my tail. She gradually relaxed, and when I ran into the kitchen for my supper, Amber crept over to Max and leaned against his leg.

'You haven't had a walk, have you?' I heard him say, and he shut the laptop.

'Where's your lead?'

Amber instantly became her joyful self again, charged into the kitchen, nearly knocking me over as I ate my tuna chunks. She circled the lounge and jumped right over the sofa, while Max was putting his coat on.

'I'm walking the dog,' he said curtly to TammyLee, and clipped the lead onto Amber's collar.

'Fine,' said TammyLee, and, once he'd gone out of the door, she muttered, 'And don't come back. I don't care if you never come back.'

I needed a wash and a long sleep. But TammyLee needed me more. She carried me upstairs, and we checked Diana, who was asleep, her face tranquil, her skin pale in the dim blue of a night light.

'Tallulah's back, Mum,' TammyLee whispered, but Diana didn't stir. 'She's on heavy medication.' TammyLee closed the door quietly and took me into her bedroom, where she kicked off her shoes and slumped onto her bed, burrowing into a mound of cushions. I stood on her chest, purring, and looked at her tormented eyes.

'I'd DIE without you, Tallulah,' she said, smoothing my coat with both hands. 'You're all I've got. And you know about Rocky.'

I did a purr-meow, to show her I understood.

'I went to Rocky's Bench after school

today,' she said. 'It's his birthday. My baby's birthday. And I'm not there for him.' She cried and cried into my fur, and I lay still and listened. 'Why did I do it, Tallulah? Why was I such a coward? What will Rocky think when he grows up, wherever he is? What will he think about his real mum dumping him like rubbish? I wish I could tell him why. I wish I could tell him that I loved him. I can't bear to think he might grow up and never know that.' She sobbed into the cushions. Then she said something that worried me a lot: 'I want to die, Tallulah. I just want ... to die.'

I felt powerless. What could one small tabby cat do, faced with a suicidal human? I patted her wet cheek with my paw, and thought maybe if I washed her face, she might feel better. So I started licking, tasting salt and make-up, licking gently round each of her eyes and calming the frown lines between them. And it worked! After a few minutes of it, she was smiling and looking at me again.

'Magic puss cat,' she said, and then she did something beautiful: she took my little black cat brush out of its drawer and began to groom my fur. I loved it, and it was just what I needed. I rolled onto my back and let her brush under my chin and down my belly. The brushing, and the appreciative purring, seemed to soothe TammyLee.

'Look at this fluff, Tallulah!' she said, showing me the wad of fur she was pulling out of the brush. She put it in a plastic bag. 'I'm saving your fur and one day I'm going to make something with it, a heart-shaped cushion, or a cushion that looks like a cat's face.' She said, 'Then I can keep you for ever, Tallulah.'

I stayed in her bedroom, thinking I'd better keep an eye on her. Instead of sleeping, I sat on the table next to her laptop, and watched her begin her homework, sighing as she ticked boxes and looked intently at the computer screen. We heard Max coming in with Amber, and he came slowly up the stairs and tapped on TammyLee's door.

She rolled her eyes.

'What?' she asked, without looking up from her work.

'Can we have a chat?' Max looked different after his walk with Amber. His cheeks were red and his eyes brighter.

'No, Dad. I'm really tired right now. And I've got homework.'

Max hovered in the doorway.

'I hoped we could make peace, and ... move on,' he said.

'Yeah, yeah, Dad.'

'I do appreciate what you do for your mum,' said Max quietly. 'I know it's not easy for you, but, for what it's worth, TammyLee, I do love you. At the end of the day, I do. And I do care about your future.'

Finally, TammyLee looked at him.

'Yeah, yeah,' she said again. 'I know you care and stuff, Dad. Look, I've got an exam tomorrow and I need to do this homework. Will you leave me alone ... PLEASE?'

Max looked upset and bewildered. Tammy-Lee sighed. She got up and gave her dad a hug. 'It's OK, Dad. I'm sorry I sounded off at you. But please ... go and watch the news or something.'

I meowed at Max and he had the sense to back off and go downstairs.

'If it wasn't for you, Tallulah, I'd go mad,' said TammyLee.

'Probably true,' I thought, and sat patiently by her laptop, pretending to doze.

'You're SUCH a good cat,' she said, and that made me feel better, especially when my angel drifted into the room and hung around by the bookshelves, shimmering with joy.

'You've done a brilliant job today, Tallulah,' she said, and I basked in the encouragement. Then she said, 'Thank you,' and covered me in stardust. My fur tingled with joy. It was the first time on this planet that someone had said thank you to me.

That weekend, I learned a lot more about the river.

Mid-morning, we set off in the hot sunshine, with Max pushing Diana's wheelchair and TammyLee in front leading Amber. A bag bulging with towels and picnic stuff was stashed in the pouch at the back of the wheelchair, and TammyLee had even put in a sachet of my favourite chicken-and-rabbit cat food, and some biscuits for Amber.

'I don't think you should let Tallulah come,' Max had said. 'We should shut her in.'

But TammyLee trusted me, and she knew how much I needed time outside.

'She's my cat, and she's not a prisoner,' she said. 'She's coming, if she wants to.'

'Don't blame me if she gets lost,' said Max.

'Tallulah can sit on my lap if she gets tired,' said Diana, her eyes luminous in her pale face. 'Come on, darling.' She patted the rug over her thin knees, and I jumped up and travelled the first bit in Diana's arms. 'We'll all look after you, Tallulah – we love you to bits.'

'It's the other way round,' I thought. 'I'm

looking after you.'

I was a happy cat now. I loved my family, I had my own dog, and I adored TammyLee. Life was just perfect now. I felt exuberant as I jumped down and chased after Amber, who had been let off the lead. We belted towards the river and I could hear laughter behind us.

'I LOVE the way that dog's tail goes round and round when she's running,' said Diana.

'She uses it as a brake,' said TammyLee. She'd got her long hair tied in a loose pony-tail at the back of her neck, and she wore a black vest with a green dragon on it. Her bangles flashed in the sun, and she had long jeans with frayed edges that brushed the floor, and a slit in each knee, which I loved to play with when she was sitting still. I'd get my paw in there, pull out a thread and play with it. Instead of her clonky shoes, she had soft sandals and she'd painted her toenails a witchy green to match the dragon. For once, she looked free and happy, snatching at seed heads of grass as we walked along.

Until a shadow fell over our day.

I'd never heard Amber growl before, but she was growling now, her soft muzzle curling to reveal the gleam of her impressive set of teeth. Her hackles were up along her spine.

'Amber!' TammyLee grabbed the dog's

collar as three young men came slouching round the corner. Amber barked, and TammyLee's aura turned to cracked glass. I figured Amber was barking at the tallest of the three lads, who was in the middle. His hair was standing up in a stiff ridge, and he had rings in his lips and eyebrows.

Alarmed by Amber's behaviour, I climbed a post and sat on top. I wanted to look at the eyes of this muscular young man who Amber didn't like. But he wasn't looking at me. He was looking at TammyLee, his eyes moving over her whole body, up and down. He and his two mates stood across the path in front of us.

Max stopped pushing the wheelchair and anger flooded his aura with a brick-red colour. He opened his mouth to speak, and Diana put a restraining hand on his arm.

'Hi, Dylan,' said TammyLee, and Amber went on growling with the sunlight glistening through her hackles.

'What's up with your dog?' Dylan asked, mockingly. 'Nasty, ain't she?'

'She doesn't like you,' said TammyLee.

'Shame about that.' Dylan still straddled the path, towering over Max, who was tutting and glaring at him.

'I thought you had a Saturday job,' said

TammyLee. 'What happened?'

Dylan shrugged. 'I quit, didn't I! Dead boring.' He put his face close to TammyLee. 'So, what happened to you then? False alarm was it?'

TammyLee looked at him steadily, her mouth twitching.

'It's none of your business,' she fired at him. 'And I don't want nothing to do with you, Dylan, so stay away from me.'

'You heard her,' said Max. 'Let us pass, please. Can't you see my wife is in a wheelchair?'

'Calm down, Pop.' Dylan grinned round at his two mates. 'I'm not planning on raping your precious daughter. Not today.' He winked at TammyLee and she glared back.

It was Diana who intervened. With a radiant smile and her eyes piercingly bright, she said, 'Good afternoon, boys, lovely to meet you. Are you enjoying this beautiful sunshine?' She held out a thin white hand. 'I'm Diana. And you are?'

Dylan got smaller and smaller as he looked at Diana's radiance. None of the boys shook the hand Diana was offering. They looked embarrassed and shuffled awkwardly from one foot to the other. Sheepishly, they moved to one side.

'Thank you. That's so kind of you.' Diana looked tenderly at each of them. 'I hope you have a lovely day. Bye-bye, now.'

Max pushed the wheelchair onwards, and Dylan turned and saw me sitting on the post. ''Ello, puss,' he said, and we had eye contact for a long moment. His eyes were turquoise and sparkly, but the sparkle was not astonishment, it was wariness, and a sense of being lost. I knew who he was instantly, by those compelling eyes. Dylan was Rocky's father.

If only I could talk.

Chapter Nine

DROPPED

Max pushed the wheelchair, until the wide path ended at a shallow place where the river bubbled over stones. Amber charged into the water with everything flapping, and I followed TammyLee onto the bank. She picked me up.

'You stay with mum, please,' she said. 'Dad and I are going swimming, just up there.' She pointed upstream to the old stone bridge where Solomon had appeared. Below it was a shining pool. The river fascinated me. I wanted to follow it into the hills and watch the waterfalls and hear its music. There were streams cascading like threads of silver down from the iron-blue ridges of the hill. I wanted to explore them, and find a tiny pool where I could sit on a stone and catch sardines. There were sheep up there too, and baby lambs who might play with me.

I was too excited to do much cuddling and purring. TammyLee put me down on Diana's lap.

'Isn't this WONDERFUL?' Diana's eyes shone. 'Oh, it's such a treat for me to see *my* river. I love it so much. Thank you for bringing me.' She reached up and pulled Max's arm until he stooped and kissed her.

'Will you be OK sitting here?' he asked. 'You can see us swimming, and when we come back and dry off, we'll have the picnic.'

'I'll be ecstatic!' said Diana, while I dough-punched with my paws in the soft blanket she had over her knees. 'And I've got Tallulah.'

TammyLee and Max stripped off their clothes down to their swimming gear, TammyLee in a bright green bikini, and Max in black swimming trunks. I sat up to watch what would happen.

'You don't have to stay with me, Tallulah,' whispered Diana. 'You go and be free and enjoy this lovely place. But come back, won't you, darling? We love you so much.'

I kissed Diana on the nose, grateful for her understanding. With my tail flying, I ran after them, along the river, keeping out of Amber's way as she was already dripping wet from nose to tail. The stone bridge was warm from the sun and I quickly found a perch out of reach of the splashes. Amber was swimming silently round and round the pool, with only her nose and eyes above the water and her tail streaming behind. Max was swimming like a frog, his chin out of the water. But TammyLee seemed transformed from the girl who marched around in clonky shoes. She was like a fish. Diving and twisting and rolling. She swam right under the water and the sunlight made webs of gold dance over her body, her hair swirled and, when she popped up for air, her face was dark pink and radiant. She looked more alive than she ever looked on land. Max soon tired and found a rock in the sun, where he sat, proudly watching his daughter. Amber clambered out and shook spirals of drops into the air, and, finally, TammyLee got out, and I stayed by myself, watching her walking back. Now was my chance to do some private hunting.

A flash of glass and a laugh caught my attention, and high up on the ridge of the hill, the three boys were sitting. One had binoculars and they were taking turns to watch TammyLee. Even though they were far away, my sensitive ears picked up a feeling of menace in their laughter, dark intention that rolled down the hillside like a rain cloud.

I looked back at the patch of sunlight where Diana sat in her wheelchair, her face lifted to the sky. My angel told me to go back to her, but first, I wanted to go up the river and explore.

So I pretended not to notice her. Only later did I get the message, for it was to be another terrible lesson. Never ignore your angel.

Under the dappled shade of trees, I followed the flowing water to a stream that joined the river. I trotted beside it, until I found a shallow fishing pool, where I sat, completely absorbed, waiting to see if any fish would come swimming into that clear water. I'd hook one out with my paw, and play with it as it jumped and flipped on the grass, and then I'd eat it, and catch another one.

My attention was so focused on the water that I ignored the footsteps and the loud voices coming down from the hillside.

'Hey, guys, that's TammyLee's cat.' It was the gruff voice of a young lad. 'Puddy Puddy Puddy,' he called, but I ignored him and wished they'd go away and leave me in peace. The tip of my tail was twitching with annoyance. If I'd been a human, I might have sworn at them.

'I'm gonna get it,' said one – Dylan.

'Nah ... leave it.'

'Who are you telling what to do? It's 'er cat, ain't it?'

'Whose?'

'The girl in the pool, stupid. TammyLee. Spoiled bitch.'

The voices got louder and louder as they argued, but I continued staring into the water, waiting for a sardine to appear.

When the footsteps came right up behind me, I swung round and put my tail up, thinking Dylan was going to stroke me. Instead, he grabbed me by the scruff and held me up in the air.

'Got 'im!' he shouted. 'D'you dare me to drop him in the river?'

'Yeah. Drop 'er cat in the river. That'll wind 'er up.'

The three of them were laughing loudly and egging each other on. They ran with me, and the boy had one hand clenching my scruff and the other gripping my back so hard his fingers were digging into my kidneys. I struggled and twisted, and flailed my claws, trying to scratch his cruel hands and make him let go of me. My nightmares came back in that moment. Joe chucking us in the hedge, Gretel throwing me out into the frosty night. 'That's what happens to bad cats,' she'd shrieked.

'Drop 'im from the bridge,' shouted one of the boys, as their shoes thudded and scuffed as they ran down to the bridge where I'd sat so happily in the sun. I was terrified. I couldn't believe they were being so cruel to me. 'Why? Why me?' My only hope was that TammyLee might rescue me.

Now Dylan was holding me up in the air above the pool.

I looked at his crazy eyes and sent him a message: 'I saved your baby's life. Don't do this to me.' But his aura had wine-red thorns like a rose in winter. He thought that dropping a cat in the river was going to cover his pain in glory. I glanced down, looking for TammyLee, but she'd gone and so had Max and Amber. My kidneys were hurting like fire, and all I wanted, as he held me over the water, was for him to let go of me – even if I was going to drown, I wanted the agony to stop. It hurt so much that I screamed and he let me go.

I fell down, down into the pool, hearing cheers and laughter and hands clapping. I hit the freezing water and went under, and the shock of it made my heart lurch painfully.

Icy water filled my mouth and rushed up my nose and into my ears. It was the worst experience of my life, even worse than the hot car. I forced my nose up and out of the water and kicked my paws the way I'd seen Amber doing. I didn't know whether cats could swim, but I tried, even though my fur was full of water and my tail felt heavy as if it would drag me under.

I hated the noise those boys were making. They were laughing at me and chanting: 'The cat's in the water! The cat's in the water!' And in the distance, TammyLee was screaming.

I swam in crazy circles, fighting the current, which was dragging me towards the weir. The pool looked vast; the banks with sun-warmed stones and grasses seemed far away. My paws got tired, I ached with the cold, my breathing was difficult as I coughed and spluttered.

I don't know where Amber came from but she hurled herself into the water; the splash threw me all over the place, my neck straining to keep my head up. Then she was swimming vigorously towards me, her eyes bright with concern. She eased her warmth alongside me, and started to push me with her nose, nearer and nearer to the bank, until I crawled out and lay there, limp and shocked, my wet tail thin and shiny like a worm.

Amber crouched down beside me, licking and whining. I heard the boys escaping, the thud-thudding of their feet and the echo of their laughter.

Then, TammyLee came running. She was crying out loud and yelling swear words at the fleeing boys.

'Poor, poor Tallulah!' She scooped me up and held me against her warm body, against the vest with the green dragon on it, and my soaking fur was dripping down her jeans. She couldn't stop crying, and Amber sat beside her, with water streaming from her coat, whining and offering her paw.

'Thank you, Amber. Thank you. You are a brilliant dog,' sobbed TammyLee, and she carried me quickly back to Max and Diana, and wrapped me in a warm towel.

'Those bastard pig boys dropped her from

the bridge,' she wept. 'How COULD they? How could they hurt Tallulah? She didn't do anything wrong.' TammyLee ranted, while I lay, shocked, wrapped in the towel on Diana's lap. Her voice rose to a scream. 'What is WRONG with the world? I don't want to stay in it. Why has some pig of a boy got to ruin the nicest day we've had for ages? They won't get away with it. I'll find the evil little jerks and chuck them in the river. In fact, I'll bloody drown them. I'll...'

'Don't be ridiculous, girl!' snapped Max. 'And stop being a drama queen.'

TammyLee turned on him: 'Don't you dare start on me. Don't you criticise me for caring. You can't tell me what to do. I'm old enough to quit school and get a job. Then who's gonna look after Mum?'

Max went white. 'I do know that,' he said, tight-lipped, 'this is not an appropriate time to raise major issues.'

I lay there, wishing they would be quiet. TammyLee was more upset than me. Diana put a kindly hand on her daughter's back as she raged and sobbed.

'Please try to calm yourself, sweetheart. Tallulah needs us to be quiet and help her recover. She needs healing, not revenge.'

TammyLee calmed down instantly, and

Max walked away, tapping at his mobile phone. 'I'm ringing the police,' he said. 'Not that they'll be interested,'

'Yes, do that,' said Diana, 'but we must focus on this poor cat. We need to get her home, and call the vet.'

'Tallulah's not strong,' said TammyLee, and her hand was still shaking as she touched me, 'because of what she went through, and look how small she is inside all that fur. Darling cat. I love her so much, Mum, I'd die for her.'

'I know, I know.' Diana was smoothing me with the towel, and TammyLee knelt on the ground beside the wheelchair, drying my face and ears with a tissue. All I felt was deep gratitude for being loved like this.

'She's purring, Mum! Listen to her.'

At home, TammyLee sat in the garden with me on her lap, helping me recover from my ordeal. The warmth of her body, and the heat of the late-afternoon sun soaked into my bones, and my fur was soon dry and silky; though it smelled of the river. I did a lot of purring, but TammyLee couldn't stop crying.

'For goodness' sake, girl,' said Max impatiently. 'The cat's all right now, surely? You've been sitting there blubbing for two hours and there's work to be done.'

'I'm not moving. Tallulah needs me. And don't call me "girl".'

The flow of healing energy from her hands came to an abrupt end, as if Max's voice had turned a switch. It wasn't the first time I'd noticed the deadening effect he had on TammyLee's spirit. She glared at Max, who stood at the kitchen door with a potato in one hand and a knife in the other.

'Can't you get supper for once?' TammyLee snarled. 'Or have you got to watch the boring old news? Again!'

'No. As it happens, I've got to do boring old work to earn us boring old money to buy boring old food and pay boring old bills!' shouted Max. He dropped the potato and it rolled, wobbling across the patio. I watched it, thinking about playing with it, and Max noticed the change in my body language.

'There you are. Look at her. She wants to play again.'

'No, she doesn't.' TammyLee scooped me into her arms and stood up. 'I'm taking her upstairs. And you don't need to PEEL POTATOES, Dad. Just get the chips out of the freezer, like the rest of us do.'

'You treat that cat like a child,' complained Max. My gaze emanated disapproval as I was carried upstairs. He couldn't know how

161

much that hurt TammyLee. How could he, when he didn't know she'd lost the child she could have loved?

TammyLee put me down on her duvet and wound a fuzzy scarf round and round me like a bird's nest. 'You stay there, Tallulah. I've got to put Mum to bed.' She sighed. 'Meow if you want me.'

I watched her go into Diana's room, and I wanted to follow her. But the warmth of the scarf was so sumptuous, and the rainbow colours of it seemed to be whirling round me. I was giddy, and the pain in my bruised kidneys was hard and sharp, as if Dylan's fingers were still clenched around my spine. Without TammyLee there, I was suddenly afraid. What if he had damaged me? What if I couldn't eat or pee? With that thought came an aftershock of pure misery. Why had that boy wanted to hurt and frighten me?

I sent out a telepathic scream to my angel, and she was there instantly, weaving her light into the rainbow scarf as she floated over the duvet.

'There is a reason,' she said. 'You have been hurt to make something happen, to help you with your mission, Tallulah.'

Grumpy and tired, I didn't respond the way you should do to an angel.

'What mission?' I growled, despite knowing perfectly well what it was.

'Remember, you came here to re-unite TammyLee with her child.'

'I wish I'd never come here.' The words heaved out of me like a cloud over the sun. It was an old familiar feeling – depression. The last time I'd had it was after Gretel left me in the car.

'If it was an accident, I could deal with it,' I said to my angel. 'But I feel it's bigger than that. I'm carrying the cruelty from across the world ... all the hurt ... it's not physical. It's coming to me from thousands of cats who've been tormented by humans.'

'Purr,' said my angel. 'Come on, purr yourself to sleep, and I will take you on a celestial journey. You will awake with new knowledge.'

'Knowledge!' I moaned, and another wave of despair engulfed my spirit. 'I never needed knowledge before. A cat knows everything it needs. But I don't know HOW I can possibly do the mission I agreed to. How can a cat manage to re-unite a mum with her baby? I can't tell TammyLee where Rocky is.'

'This knowledge will be given in spirit,' said my angel. 'Now, do as I asked. Purr.'

My first purr came out as a complaint,

and it hurt right through my body.

'Listen,' said my angel. 'Listen to the shining cats purring out there in another dimension.'

Relaxing a little, I listened, and, at first, heard only a murmur of voices from Diana's room, and, from downstairs, the sound of Amber's tail banging against the fridge and the snip-snip of scissors as Max cut off bits of bacon for her.

My angel began to hum a lullaby to me and a delicious drowsiness melted my pain into slumber. In my sleep, I heard the heavenly purring, saw the thistledown faces of spirit cats, their eyes like lamps burning around me, illuminating my dreams with an incandescence that was both healing and inviting.

'Am I dying?' I asked, but there was no answer except the humming, the purring and the whirling colours of the scarf. My angel kept repeating something like a mantra: 'There is a reason, a reason...' Her words became a cushion of stars, carrying me high above the house and the garden, above the river and the hills, then through the sky, faster and faster. So fast that the stillness of my sleep was tightly tucked around me, keeping me safe.

My spirit was intact, yet I felt like two cats

who were separating. One was flying gloriously through endless sparkles, the other was lying limp and lifeless on TammyLee's bed. From some distant place, I watched TammyLee come back into her bedroom and look closely at that tabby-and-white cat. 'That's me,' I thought. 'But I'm not supposed to die yet.'

Her long fingers slipped through my fur, the witchy-green nails shining. Her hand was suddenly still and she seemed to be listening, her face going pale like one of the cream roses in the garden.

'Don't die on me, Tallulah,' she whispered. 'Please, Tallulah.'

I saw the panic in her eyes, but I was detached, still in that distant starry place, no longer flying, but floating, closer and closer to the sequinned edges of my true home, the spirit world, where I was the Queen of Cats. Why had I ever left? I yearned to go back.

'Why can't I go in?' I asked my angel.

'It is not your time,' she replied, and I searched her silver eyes for an explanation. 'You are a brave cat, a bright spirit and you CAN complete your mission. Help is on the way. Feel the hand that is touching you.'

I focussed on TammyLee's hand and it was trembling as she caressed the silky fur over my heart. She lay down and put her ear against me, the bobble of her earring pressing into me. She was listening for a heartbeat.

'Purr,' said my angel, but I couldn't. I gazed at her. In her full colours, she was dazzling. 'You are very ill, but remember, there is a healer for you. She gave you your name, Tallulah.'

A face drifted into my mind, manifesting through the web of stars, the girl with the long dark plait and the blazing light: Roxanne!

'Send out the call,' said my angel. 'And she will come.'

'I can't,' I said. 'I can't even purr.'

'You can. You can think. And thinking has power. Think of Roxanne. Hold her face in your dreams. Tell her you need help.'

'But it doesn't work like that with humans,' I argued.

'Thinking has power. Just do it.'

I held Roxanne's face in my mind, tightly in my dreams as the angel had said. At the same time I watched the pandemonium in the house as TammyLee flew into a panic. She carried me downstairs.

'Dad... DO something. She's dying.'

'Don't be RIDICULOUS.'

'WHY can't you believe me, Dad?'

Max came and looked at my limp body, and Amber came creeping along the floor, whimpering. I felt Max change from being angry to being the organiser.

'Put her in the car. We'll take her to the vet. Now,' he said. 'It might not be too late.'

I didn't want to go in a car. I hated the vet. But I had no choice. Limp and hardly breathing, I could only be in TammyLee's arms as Max quickly locked the house door, got in and revved the engine, the wheels scrunching on gravel.

'Focus on the healer,' said my angel, and I held Roxanne in my mind.

'Who are you phoning?' Max asked sharply, as TammyLee tapped at her mobile in the car. 'Damn these bloody traffic lights, they're always bloody well red. Come on. Come on.'

Cats do believe in miracles. I'd forgotten about them. But one was happening right now in the back of Max's speeding car.

'Roxanne,' said TammyLee.

She was phoning Roxanne. My angel was right! I'd sent out the call in my thoughts, and it must have arrived.

I heard Roxanne's voice come through the phone. A mobile phone is a bit crude, but it's the nearest thing humans have to real telepathy.

'Penny from Cat's Protection gave me your number,' explained TammyLee, half talking, half crying. 'Do you remember a tabby-and-white fluffy cat? Tallulah?'

'Of course! Beautiful Tallulah. I'm tuning into her right now,' replied Roxanne. 'What's happened?'

'These EVIL boys got hold of her and threw her ... threw her...' TammyLee couldn't speak for the sobs of rage gusting through her as she remembered my ordeal.

'Take a deep breath,' said Roxanne.

'In the river,' TammyLee said. 'We're taking her to the vet right now. But it's more than that, Roxanne ... it ... it's deep emotional stuff ... the hell of being bullied ... and, God knows, I should understand THAT.' She took another gulp of air.

'Can we not have another drama when I'm driving?' Max asked wearily.

'She's my best friend,' explained Tammy-Lee, ignoring Max. 'She didn't do anything. We got her out and dried her off, but I'm frightened they've hurt her in some other way ... b ... broken her back or something terrible ... she hasn't walked or put her tail up, and she's gone limp.'

'I'm not getting that,' said Roxanne. 'I'm sensing she's bruised and shocked ... see what the vet has to say and I'll come over when you've got her home. Where do you live?'

'Oh, thanks, Roxanne. River Cottage, just off the big roundabout by the park. Thanks, you're a star!'

The next thing I knew was the smell of the vet's place, the wailing of cats in cages in the waiting room, the cold of the table they put me on. The fear and the silence while he examined me with gentle hands, pulling each paw, checking my tail, squeezing my sore tummy. When he did that, it hurt and I heard myself let out a long mewling cry.

'She's bruised,' he said. 'Her legs are OK but she doesn't want to stand up, does she? We'll do a scan.'

While he was running the scanner over me, I could feel Roxanne coaxing me back from where I still hovered, gazing longingly into the spirit world.

'I think she's basically OK,' the vet said, 'but shock can affect cats very badly ... worse than a human. I'll give her a mild sedative and she'll sleep for a few hours. Take her home and keep her warm.'

I opened my eyes then and saw Tammy-

Lee's anxious face, and the glint of her bangles as she stroked me gently under the chin.

I remembered how much I loved her and I was so pleased to see her there, looking after me, that I managed a purr-meow.

'Magic puss cat,' she said, and smiled at me.

I was back.

The long sleep did me good, and, when I awoke, I found myself back on the bed with the rainbow scarf wound around me, and TammyLee was bringing Roxanne into the bedroom.

The two girls sat one each side of me and I felt as if the sun itself had come into the room. I wanted to love them both, so I stood up, stretched, and wove my way to and fro between them, rubbing my head against them, my tail brushing their bare arms.

'She's much better,' said TammyLee. 'Listen to her purring. Maybe she doesn't need healing now.'

'We'll see,' said Roxanne, and she picked me up and held me against her heart. 'Sometimes, animals want to talk to me. I can hear their voices by telepathy.'

'Can you? Wow! What do you want me to do?'

'Just be here ... and listen. If she wants me to, I'll tell you what she's saying. Please be very still and quiet.'

As before, Roxanne closed her eyes and talked to me in a language I understood: telepathy. First, we talked about the boys dropping me in the river and whether I hated them for it.

'She's telling me about the boys,' said Roxanne out loud, 'and we're forgiving them.'

'I shan't,' said TammyLee, and her eyes burned. 'I'll never forgive them. Never.'

'Animals do,' said Roxanne. 'They forgive us and forgive us, no matter how many mistakes we make.'

'But those evil jerks don't deserve forgiveness.'

'But you do. You deserve to do the forgiving. It heals you. You are letting go of a burden,' said Roxanne.

TammyLee looked confused. 'No one's ever said that to me before,' she said, frowning. 'I can't get my head round it.'

'It's your heart that needs to forgive, not your head,' said Roxanne, in a quiet, hypnotic voice. 'Your heart is full of love and light. There's no room in it for hatred and blame.'

'So ... how do you do it?'

'You just let go, my darling. Like a big stone you have carried up a steep mountain ... it's been dragging you down ... but now, let it go and watch it rolling away, and you feel light and free as a bird.'

She spoke passionately, and TammyLee listened intently, shaking her head a little.

'Now, if you don't mind, I'm going to listen to Tallulah,' said Roxanne, and both girls kept still and quiet. Overjoyed to have a listener, I told Roxanne everything. How I, the Queen of Cats, had come here to re-unite a mother with her baby, how I had found Rocky and kept him warm, as a tiny baby. Then, how I'd found him again and didn't know how I could convey information to TammyLee. I asked Roxanne to tell her.

What I didn't expect was the shattering effect it would have on TammyLee.

Chapter Ten

NEVER, NEVER, EVER

Roxanne was hesitating to speak the words I'd given her. She was trying to change its meaning. I sighed and patted her face with my paw.

'So, what is Tallulah telling you?' asked TammyLee, her eyes wide open and thirsty for the information.

'She's ... giving me a name...' said Roxanne, carefully, and she put a hand on TammyLee's arm.

'A name? What name?'

'Rocky.'

TammyLee stiffened, her aura turning to hard bright steel, like a suit of armour.

'So ... what about Rocky?' she asked after a long pause.

'I ... I'm not sure I should tell you ... it ... well ... it might be painful for you, darling,' said Roxanne kindly, and I gave her concerned face another pat – 'but Tallulah wants me to. It's important to her, and she's been frustrated because she can't tell you.'

'Tell me what?'

I paid attention to the intense eye contact between the two women, and the way TammyLee looked like a child on the edge of a stormy sea, afraid, but wanting to go in.

'Tallulah is the Queen of Cats in the spirit world,' said Roxanne. 'Are you comfortable with that kind of stuff?'

'Yeah ... I mean ... well, she would be, wouldn't she?' TammyLee smiled. 'I always knew she was magic.'

I stepped gently on to her lap, and curled up there, doing the most calming kind of purr I could muster. She had to listen. I would keep her still and quiet.

'Is that it then?' asked TammyLee.

'No ... there's more ... about Rocky.'

'Go on.'

'Tallulah wants you to know she saved Rocky's life when he was a tiny baby. She stayed all night with him and kept him warm.'

TammyLee gasped. I looked at her eyes and they were flooded with fear that seemed to be erupting from some deep dark well in her soul. I cuddled close.

'There's more,' said Roxanne. 'This cat is like a guardian angel.'

'Go on.'

'Tallulah came here to support you, TammyLee. She adores you. And ... and...'

'Oh, I know that. I adore her.'

TammyLee relaxed for a second, and took a deep breath. Roxanne was still staring at her intently, and, in the moment of silence, I could hear Amber coming upstairs. Her nails clicked along the landing and she peeped round the door.

'Aw ... look at that,' said Roxanne. 'Is this Amber? Isn't she beautiful? She's come to love you.'

Amber sidled up to TammyLee and sat down, leaning her warm bulk against her legs.

'She knows,' said TammyLee, stroking the dog's silky ears.

'Animals do. They know, and they forgive, and they don't judge us.'

'So ... what else did Tallulah tell you?'

'She wants you to know that she has found Rocky, and, when the time is right, she will lead you to him.'

I'd thought TammyLee would be pleased, but she wasn't. She went white. Her eyes hardened and she stood up and put me back on Roxanne's lap. She looked at the window, and the door and up at the ceiling. Then she

175

stalked over to the open door, slammed it shut and turned to face us, leaning against it. Her knees were shaking and her green eyes shone like the river water.

'Don't tell my dad,' she pleaded in a whisper, 'or my mum. Or anyone. If you tell anyone about Rocky, I'll kill myself. I mean it.'

She was shaking so hard it made the door rattle. We all looked at her ... Roxanne, Amber and me ... and in that moment, I saw TammyLee's angel holding her in a cocoon of misty light, and the angel looked sad.

'Don't worry ... I won't.' Roxanne didn't look surprised at all.

'Thanks.' TammyLee moved away from the door and went to the mirror. She started coiling her hair into a bun and wiping the smudges off her checks with a round white pad she took from a pot. 'I've been in such a state all day,' she said, 'and I've got my GCSE maths exam on Monday and my mum to look after. I've gotta get my act together. I have to stay functional ... I can't fall apart.' She leaned close to the mirror and brushed mascara onto her eyelashes, acting as if she didn't care and didn't want us around.

'I'd better go.' Roxanne gave me a kiss and put me down next to Amber.

'Yeah ... thanks, Roxanne. Appreciate it,'

said TammyLee, but she didn't glance up from the mirror.

'I'll come again if you need me.'

'Cool. Might do.'

'Are you sure you're OK?'

'Yeah ... I'm good.'

After Roxanne had gone, TammyLee came over to the bed and looked at it. She smoothed the quilt, and then collapsed, curled up in a ball and went to sleep almost instantly. Amber wasn't supposed to go on the bed but she climbed up there and stretched out against TammyLee's back, and I curled up with my head on her chest. The three of us slept and slept until it was dark, and, when Max put his head round the door, I stared at him until he went away.

We all needed to sleep, and let the day fold up into the night like a damaged flower, best forgotten.

I was better in the morning, well enough to go downstairs, eat my breakfast and sit in the window in the morning sun. It looked as if everything was back to normal, until Max had a go at TammyLee.

We were out on the patio, and TammyLee had her face in a mug of coffee, with a maths book spread out on the garden table. Amber was rolling on the lawn, and Diana sat in her wheelchair, drinking from a funny little cup with gold squiggles on it. I sat quietly on the cushion next to TammyLee, dreaming of the time when we could go to the river again and I could resume my sardine fishing.

Then Max's aura caught my attention. He was on guard, like a dog, tense and suspicious. His coffee sat untouched on the table, his newspaper folded on his lap, and he was staring into the sky, then glancing at TammyLee with questions simmering in his eyes. He kept taking a breath, as if to speak, then changing his mind.

'That boy...' he said, eventually. 'What was his name again?'

'Dylan,' said TammyLee, without looking up. 'And I'm trying to revise, Dad.'

'Do you know him?' asked Max, his eyes bright with suspicion.

'Yeah. He was a year ahead of me in school. He's left now, Dad.'

'So what's he doing now?'

TammyLee shrugged. 'How should I know?'

'I don't like his attitude,' said Max, frowning.

'He's just a lad,' said Diana. 'You were like that once.'

'I most certainly was not. I'd never have dared speak to an adult like he did. Rude, he was, and arrogant. If there's one thing I abhor, its insolence.'

'Oh, don't go on about it, Dad. I'm trying to study.'

Max stood up and banged his newspaper on the table.

'Answer my question, girl.'

TammyLee sighed. 'I don't know,' she repeated edgily. 'And you're being rude, calling me "girl".'

'Well, I didn't like the way he spoke to you, or the way he looked at you. He openly threatened you. Didn't you hear what he said?'

'Look, Dad, it's pretty typical. All mouth and trousers,' said TammyLee.

'Well, I hope you haven't been associating with him.'

TammyLee glared at Max. 'Who I make friends with is my business, not yours. And, in case you haven't noticed, I've got an EXAM tomorrow. You just don't listen, do you?'

'She has,' said Diana. 'I think you should leave this for another time, Max. We had enough drama yesterday. Let's have some peace.'

'You can't have peace when there are issues to be discussed,' said Max. His back was rigid, his cheeks twitching as he looked at TammyLee, who was doing her best to ignore him. I just sat quietly, looking at the dark pink colour that was creeping up TammyLee's neck and over her face. I wished Max would leave her alone. Amber was thinking the same, her brown eyes moving anxiously from one to the other.

'Leave it for now, Max,' Diana insisted. Her face was white, her eyes like black bubbles, and her hands looked luminous, as if she was made of glass. I sensed that she was very ill. Like me, she had been to the distant shores of the spirit world, and returned, many times.

'All right. For now.' Max picked up his newspaper and shook it open. He glowered at TammyLee. 'If you didn't speak to me so rudely, young lady, I'd be more prepared to listen.'

TammyLee rolled her eyes and Diana put a hand on her arm. A secret smile passed between them. I wondered what would happen when she died. Would TammyLee leave? Would she take me with her?

I'd met some cats who lived their whole lives in one place, with one family, and they were contented. They didn't know how lucky they were. You'd think that I, the Queens of Cats, would be given a life of luxury and stability. But so far, my life had been full of change and anxiety. I wasn't sure I could cope with much more of it.

Only Amber knew when I was anxious. Now, she put her paws up on the window-sill, her tail wagging, and gazed at me with shining eyes. I gave her a kiss, and jumped down to sit close to her warm comforting body. We were best mates, Amber and I, no matter what the humans were doing. My bond with her was precious.

TammyLee was trying to focus on her exam, but I sensed that Rocky was uppermost in her mind. When she came home from school, I ran to meet her, and she seemed happy.

'That's IT!' she said joyfully, as she picked me up. 'The last exam is over. I've made a mess of it, but I don't really care, Tallulah. I'm going to be a hairdresser, no matter what Dad says.'

She carried me up to her bedroom and I sat, looking at her, waiting. I knew what was lurking under the joy. Sadness, guilt and a mother's grief at losing her child.

'It has to come out,' my angel had said, 'and you must be there.'

So I sat, and looked into her soul, and waited.

The exams were over. TammyLee had a space in front of her, and, like a summer sky, it darkened in seconds with the thundercloud of emotions she'd been suppressing for the last year.

'You know ... about Rocky, Tallulah,' she whispered, and started twisting her bangles round and round her arm, pinching them together and letting them fall, clinking and twinkling down to her wrist. 'I think about him every day,' she said. 'It's like ... he'll never leave me alone, Tallulah. I ... I so wish I'd cuddled him ... he was gorgeous ... he had such bright, knowing eyes ... and cute little hands that looked like mine... How could I have done what I did? He'll never forgive me and I'll never forgive myself. I'm so wicked, Tallulah ... thank you for loving me... I don't deserve you. Oh, what am I going to do?'

She cried out as the storm of remorse broke into her summer. It was loud, and unstoppable. I heard Amber whining and padding upstairs, her tail down as she came round the door and sat close, her chin on the bed. Then I heard the tap and shuffle of Diana's Zimmer frame as she dragged herself into TammyLee's bedroom, her eyes brimming with concern.

'What is it, darling?'

TammyLee shook her head violently. 'I can't tell you, Mum.'

'You can, just take your time.' Diana manoeuvred herself onto TammyLee's bed, and took her daughter's hot head into her frail arms, stroking her back and twiddling strands of her hair, which were escaping from the fiercely pinned bun.

TammyLee tore at it and shook it loose. 'I can't STAND my hair, it's driving me bonkers and I'm too hot,' she moaned, and Diana picked up a magazine and began to fan her daughter's face with it.

'But what's really wrong?' she asked. 'Something's been bugging you for a long, long time, TammyLee ... don't think I haven't noticed. It's OK, love, you know you can tell me anything... I won't tell your Dad... I promise.'

'I can't.' TammyLee shook her head. She stared at Diana. 'You shouldn't have got out of bed, Mum. I'll get your tea now and sort you out.'

'No, sweetheart, I don't need anything and I'm going to sit here until you tell me what's wrong,' said Diana. 'I can't bear to see you suffer like this. Tallulah's all right now. Your exams are over. So what is it?'

TammyLee was silent, her fingers pulling a long gold thread out of a cushion.

'Is it ... looking after me?' Diana asked, and TammyLee shook her head, her eyes staring out of the window.

'As long as I'm alive, you'll never be free,' said Diana seriously. 'I worry for you. It's not the kind of life I dreamed of for my only daughter. I dreamed of you being happy. Growing up and meeting a lovely young man, and, eventually ... grandchildren! I'd so love to be a granny.'

'Oh, Mum!' TammyLee pulled harder at the long golden thread she was extracting from a cushion. She wound it tightly round her fingers and seemed to be holding her breath. Obviously, Diana's comment had made things worse. The silence went on so long that I felt I should meow, and, when I did, they both looked at me. I could see the desperation in TammyLee's eyes, and I wanted to help. Moving softly, I crept onto her lap and stretched my paws over her heart. But still she was silent, and I tried so hard to communicate telepathically with Diana.

Something must have got through, for Diana was looking intently at her daughter, trying to get eye contact.

'What is it, darling?' she asked. Then, in the long silence, Diana reached out her hand to touch TammyLee's shoulder. 'You're not ... not...?' She took a deep breath. 'You're not pregnant, are you love? You know I'd stand by you if you were.'

'No, Mum. It's OK. You don't have to give me the birds-and-bees stuff.'

'Promise?'

'Promise.'

'Well, are you going to unpick that whole cushion?' Diana's eyes danced with gentle humour. 'Or shall we start on the sofa?'

TammyLee smiled.

'You're amazing, Mum,' she said, and the tension had passed ... until the next time, I thought. One day, TammyLee will tell Diana about Rocky.

But later, when I was curled up on her bed, TammyLee whispered to me fiercely: 'Mum and Dad must never know about Rocky. Never, never, EVER.'

Chapter Eleven

DYLAN

It didn't take me long to recover from being dropped in the river. I had a happy home, and lots of love and attention. TammyLee spoiled me with the best food, and a fishy tasting tablet she gave me daily. 'For your coat,' she said, and my tabby and white fur was thick and glossy. She brushed me a lot, so I didn't have the hassle of sorting out matted tufts of hair. She examined my paws, and my eyes, and even my teeth, to make sure I was healthy. I couldn't have been a more pampered cat.

I responded by showing the family how to have fun. I didn't need TV or a computer. A cardboard box was my favourite, and TammyLee made one with little doors and holes I could pop in and out of and dark corners where I could hide toys and treasures. That summer, I developed a lot of new skills. Like opening zips on handbags. A zip made me dance with excitement if it had a toggle I could pull. The fun was in discovering the amazing stuff inside handbags ... soft things and shiny things. Lipstick cases were what I liked. Those were fantastic to chase across the floor and under the sofa.

Best of all were the squeals of laughter from visitors when I cheekily opened a new handbag, put my paw inside and took things out. If there was a money purse, I pulled it out between my teeth, as if it was a piece of chicken, and that always raised the loudest laugh. Then I circled round it, working out how to get it open, and I usually succeeded. The pound coins were brilliant for batting across the polished wood floor. I meowed at TammyLee, until she picked one up and cleverly made it spin or roll for me to chase. But after one incident, I wasn't allowed the bits of crackly paper. I'd shredded a banknote and even Amber had disapproved.

'You're pushing your luck,' she said. 'I used to chew shoes and books if I could get one, and once, Max actually growled at me, as if he wanted to be a dog, and he smacked me with his newspaper. Money, and shoes, and books are important to humans.'

Summer rolled on, and Amber and I were carefree and happy. TammyLee was on holiday, and she took us out every day to the park and along the river.

I still loved the river, despite my ordeal, but now I was very, very wary. The sound of boys' voices made me hide, or run to TammyLee, who could carry me. Amber chased any dogs who barked at me, and I soon worked out a route high in the trees, as if I were a monkey, running and leaping through the branches. It was great.

I hoped that one day, we would meet Kaye and Rocky. I watched women with push-chairs from my perches in the trees. I planned to go racing over to them, and sit on Rocky's lap. Then TammyLee would have to collect me, and she'd meet Rocky.

But it didn't happen. Kay and Rocky were nowhere to be seen.

Everywhere we went on those days of golden sun, TammyLee carried in her heart the shadow of her lost baby, and the guilt of what she had done. It was hard for me to keep believing I could bring them together.

'There is a plan,' my angel said. 'You don't need to do anything, Tallulah. The love you are giving is precious and healing for TammyLee.'

I'd established a place in the garden where I talked to my angel regularly. It was under an apple tree, where I often settled down in the dappled sunlight to sleep and to listen to the buzz of wasps clustered around the fallen apples.

'Watch the swallows,' my angel said, 'and when you see them gathering on the wires, they are leaving and, this autumn, everything will change, not just for you, but for the whole community. There will be a time of change, a time when you must stay indoors, away from the river.'

'Why?' I asked, puzzled. 'I like the river and so does Amber.'

'It looks tranquil now,' said my angel, 'but in the winter it will roar like a lion, and the water will be tawny gold and foaming, like the mane of a lion.'

'But why?'

'Because it will be winter.'

Winter. I remembered winter in Gretel's garden. The soil knobbly and locked together with ice crystals so that I couldn't scratch it up when I needed to. The lawn with blue shadows on crisp white grass. The trees coated in ice. The birds desperate and hungry, easy to catch. What did winter have to do with a lion?

'Be happy while you can,' said my angel. 'Before the winter, TammyLee will have something very hard to deal with. It could go either way … like when you were ill, you were caught in the golden land between life and death, a land that sparkles and sustains, but sends you back to live your life and do the task you agreed. Believe me, TammyLee will need your love.'

'So … lots of purring, and stay away from the river. Is that it?' I asked.

'That's it, for now.'

Soon after I had watched the swallows leaving on their long journey, I noticed a change in TammyLee's routine.

She had started college, part-time, training to be a hairdresser.

'Wasting your life. Wasting it,' Max ranted at her. 'Doing people's HAIR, for goodness' sake. Subscribing to vanity. When you were bright enough to go to university.'

At first, TammyLee argued with him, but mostly she rolled her eyes and ignored him.

'I can't wait to get away from Dad,' she told me in private, 'get my own flat and have some peace. I only stay here because of Mum. She needs me, and I love her, Tallulah. I wish she could get better.'

One day, I had a terrible shock. I'd been off on my own all afternoon, catching mice, exploring other people's gardens and going through their cat flaps. I could tell from the shadows that it was time for the college bus to bring TammyLee home. So I hurried back. Instead of going under the gate, I climbed the high wooden fence, intending to sit up there and watch for the bus.

I looked down into the garden, and a pair of insolent eyes were staring back at me. Sitting under the apple tree was a young man dressed in black, his bare shoulders gleaming in the sun. He was eating an apple from the tree in loud bites.

I froze. It was HIM. Sitting in *our* garden, in MY favourite spot. What was he doing there?

Fear and anger kinked and coiled like two snakes in my mind. While he was there, I didn't dare to jump down from the fence and I wanted to go through the cat flap and get my tea. I couldn't go home!

He looked up at me, and I saw guilt in his eyes. 'Glad you survived,' he said, and when I stared stonily back, he added: 'I'm sorry, puss ... sorry I did that to you... I ain't gonna 'urt you now. I've changed, see? Come on, get down.' He clicked his fingers. 'Puddy puddy puddy...'

I understood that cats were often addressed as 'Pussy', which was OK ... but 'Puddy' was

191

so insulting to my status as Tallulah. I added contempt to my stony stare.

With a casual flick of his wrist, he chucked the apple core against the fence with a bang. The red and white pieces scattered into a clump of asters, upsetting bees and butter-flies who were gathering nectar.

I wasn't prepared to trust him, and I had a quick decision to make. Should I run down the road to meet TammyLee? Or save myself from this monster who had dropped me in the river? I knew I could move faster than he could, but I was still scared that he would cross the lawn in long strides and snatch me from the fence. I had to get out of his reach.

I crawled along the fence like a caterpillar, my tail down, my claws clinging. Instinct made me move stealthily, so that nothing would want to chase me. One paw at a time, I reached the end of the fence where it adjoined the house. I scrambled up some ivy and onto the roof. I'd never been on the roof, so I picked my way over the tiles, which were prickly with lichen. Flicking my ears back to catch any sound from Dylan, I walked to the high ridge of the roof, stretched myself over a nicely rounded, sunbaked tile, and pretended to wash. It wouldn't do to let that boy see I was intimidated by him. Washing was the ultimate put-down, and a good way of observing him without seeming to do so.

He looked smaller, down there on the lawn, and kind of lonely. Why was he there? Was he waiting for TammyLee? And why wasn't Amber barking? Then I remembered that, earlier in the day, Max had gone off in the car with Diana in the front seat and Amber wagging her tail in the back. So I was alone in the place.

From the roof, there was a view of the road and the river glinting between the trees. I resolved to spend more time on this lovely roof, despite being dive-bombed by two jackdaws who didn't appreciate having me on their patch. Glancing down at Dylan sitting under the apple tree, I found myself fascinated by his aura. Unlike when I first encountered him, it was now unexpectedly bright. Mostly blue and green with an outer edge of gold. Being a healing cat, I examined it in some detail, looking first at the area where his heart would be, and it was dark with pain.

I saw that Dylan was carrying the loneliness of anger.

He was so angry that the friends he needed wouldn't go near him.

'You are doing brilliantly, Tallulah.' The voice startled me, and I was surprised to see my angel on the roof with me. I'd been so focused on Dylan.

'Just don't ask me to go down there,' I said.

'I never ask you to do something unless I know you can,' said my angel. In that moment, my spiritual vision was full on, and even the trees had webs of light around them. I gazed at my angel, remembering that she was the Angel of Secrets.

'Is something going to happen?' I asked.

'Wait and see. Sit up and look majestic,' she advised. 'And remember... Dylan has an angel too.'

I fluffed my fur and sat up, aware of the radiance around me and the sunlight shining on my white chest, my eyes golden and alert.

TammyLee paused at the garden gate, staring at Dylan sitting under the apple tree. Her face hardened with rage, and she burst through the gate in a fury.

'What the HELL are YOU doing here?'

Dylan didn't move. Only his foot started to tap-tap at the grass. His eyes burned blue as he looked steadily at TammyLee.

'GET THE HELL OUT of my garden!' she screamed, and flew at him like a fighting cat, attacking him with her bag. It glittered wildly as she swung it at his head. Dylan put his hands up to defend himself, but he didn't fight back.

'Calm down, will you?' he said.

'Don't tell ME to calm down. What are you doing here? And where's my cat? You'd better not have hurt her. If you touch my cat EVER AGAIN, I'll bloody kill you. Get the FUCK out of our garden.'

She swung the bag at his head and her precious mobile flew out and landed on the lawn. She snatched it up. 'I'm phoning my Dad, if you don't go.'

Dylan's eyes were so powerful that when he turned them to look at something, everyone else would look at it too. So TammyLee followed his stare, and saw me sitting majestically on the roof. I meowed at her.

'The cat's OK, see? I ain't touched 'er,' said Dylan.

TammyLee had her keys in her hand and I could see she was working out whether to run into the house and slam the door, or run away, or stay there. She stood glowering down at Dylan, her boots planted wide apart, her hair twinkling with skeins of tiny stars she had woven into it.

'You know I do kick-boxing,' she said, 'and I don't want to have to use it on you.'

'Yeah. It don't faze me, babe.'

'And don't call me "babe".'

Dylan stretched out his hand to her. 'Will you sit down? Please, TammyLee. For five minutes? I didn't come here to make trouble. I got something to say to you. Please?'

'Why should I?'

'Why shouldn't you? Don't worry, I ain't gonna touch you, babe. I'm just asking you to listen. Please, TammyLee. I promise I'll go away, if you'll just hear what I have to say.' He lowered his voice and it was barely audible.

'Go closer,' said my angel. 'Be brave, Tallulah. TammyLee needs you.'

When I saw TammyLee sit down on the grass beside Dylan, I meowed, and made my way down the roof. There was a silence as both of them watched me make a scary jump onto the fence.

'Tail up,' said my angel, and I managed that as well. But I wasn't going to jump down into the garden.

TammyLee got up and came to fetch me. I cuddled into her, purring and kissing her hot face, but I was tense with fear as she sat down next to Dylan.

'Go on then ... say it,' she demanded.

'Look... I'm sorry.' Dylan's eyes looked down at the ground. 'I don't know what got into me that day. I apologise, unreservedly, for what I did to the cat. I don't suppose you'll ever forgive me … but there you are, I've said sorry and it wasn't easy.'

'Hearts and flowers!' said TammyLee, sarcastically. 'Why don't you say sorry to the cat? She's called Tallulah, and she's a rescue cat and she … she's my best mate.'

Dylan nodded. He tried to make eye contact with me, but I refused it. He tried to touch my fur, but when I felt his finger, I tensed. My claws dug into TammyLee's pink top. I stopped purring and growled like a dog.

'She doesn't trust you. Best leave her alone,' said TammyLee, and she stroked me until I relaxed. 'If you knew what she's been through, you wouldn't have been so cruel, Dylan. And look what you've lost … the love and friendship of a beautiful cat. That's something precious to me.'

'Yeah, I get it.' Dylan tore a leaf from a nearby plant and began to shred it. 'Pity you don't feel the same about babies.'

TammyLee stiffened. 'What d'you mean by that? I love little children.'

Dylan raised his eyebrows. He was ominously silent for another painful minute. We all listened to my purring, and the chattering of sparrows. We watched a butterfly feeding on a rotten apple, its wings like jewels in the dappled sunlight. Under my paws, Tammy-Lee's heart began to thud at double its normal speed.

Then Dylan dropped his bombshell.

'I want to know what happened, Tammy-Lee. What happened to our baby?'

'What baby?' she fired, lifting her chin defiantly. I could feel the lies queuing up in her mind.

'Don't pretend you don't know,' Dylan insisted, his voice quiet.

'I don't know.'

'The baby we made together, that day we skived off the school harvest festival. Come on, TammyLee ... you told me at the end of term that you were pregnant. Come on, admit it.'

TammyLee was holding me with one hand and ripping up blades of grass with the other. She pursed her lips and refused to look at Dylan.

'Look, I know I did a stupid thing,' he said, 'when you said you were pregnant I couldn't get my head round it and I walked away. And you screamed after me. Remember? You said you never wanted to see me again.'

'I was fourteen, and I didn't want sex with you, Dylan.'

'Oh, come on, yes, you did.'

'I DID NOT. You just got me drunk with that bottle of stuff you said was only cider. Then you took advantage of me because you knew I hadn't got a life 'cause I look after my mum. I could have reported you for rape, but I didn't.'

'No, you just dumped me, didn't you?' Dylan's eyes darkened with pain. 'One minute you were crazy about me, telling everyone I was hot, and the next minute you were acting like I never existed. It hurt. I know I act the hard man and stuff, but I do have feelings, and I actually did love you.'

'Is that why you dropped my cat in the river?'

'No ... I s'pose I just wanted to hurt you back somehow.'

There was another painful silence. I shuffled around and put my chin on Tammy-Lee's heart so that she could feel my loud purring. But I didn't want to be there, in the middle of this fierce argument. I wanted to be in the kitchen, eating my tea in peace. I wanted to curl up on Amber's bed and wait for her to come back and lie with me, and tell me about her trip to the beach.

'I respected you, for the way you look after your mum,' Dylan said, 'but I don't have a home life and stuff like you. I live in a no-hopers' flat and I've only got my mum and she's pissed off with me most of the time. That day, when you told me you were pregnant, I was really immature. I got to thinking about it later, and actually dreaming about being a dad.'

TammyLee was quieter now. She was listening to him, and stroking me along my back and rubbing behind my ears with her fingers.

'I watched you,' continued Dylan, 'all those months, and you were getting a bump. You just wore loose clothes and told everyone you were bingeing on junk food.'

'So?'

'So what happened? What happened to OUR baby? TammyLee, I'm not leaving until you tell me.'

'I miscarried.' TammyLee spat the words out like a tablet she couldn't swallow.

Dylan stood up, and so did she, still holding me.

'I ... don't ... believe you,' he said, forcefully, and his eyes narrowed.

'Suit yourself.'

He took a step forward and put his face close to us. I felt TammyLee begin to tremble.

'Get this, you lying bitch,' Dylan hissed. 'I

intend to find out what you really did. I know when our baby should have been born ... round about the eighteenth of May, I reckon. I read the papers, see? And I watch the news. I can find it all online ... and if I find out you dumped him somewhere, I'll take a DNA test, and YOU are going to take responsibility for what you did to MY baby. No one messes with me, or my family.'

With a final glare of his blue eyes, he left the garden in three strides, vaulted the gate into the road, and we listened to the thud-thud of his footsteps going away.

TammyLee was cold and shaking all over. She cried into my fur.

'Oh, God, Tallulah. What am I going to DO?'

Chapter Twelve

A DARK AFTERNOON

I first encountered Dylan's mum on a dark autumn afternoon. The leaves were falling in shoals, blowing along the road and piling into corners and gateways. I was sitting in a nest I'd made in the hedge, a cosy hiding place near the gate. I'd come outside for some thinking time, leaving the family clustered round the television, watching weather reports.

'There's now a red alert for prolonged, heavy rain,' Max had said. 'I'd better go and get some sandbags. We don't want the river in the garden again.'

I didn't know what he meant. I asked Amber, and she didn't know either. But I remembered what my angel had said about the river being like a lion in the winter, and it made me uneasy. My instinctive attunement to the natural world gave me a sense of something ominous, a massive storm prowling out over the sea. I could feel its shadow, and taste its salt on the wind.

TammyLee had been full of anxiety since Dylan's visit. Yet she continued to look after Diana and clean the house with breathtaking efficiency. She seemed able to flick a switch and suddenly become calm and cheerful, and proud of her ability to be her mum's carer. She told no one, except me, of her private torment over Rocky.

'Every day of my life, I think about Rocky,' she often said, 'and every day I hate myself for what I did. I might never see him again in my whole life, and I want to, so much. Supposing I couldn't ever have another baby? And I'm so scared, Tallulah, you're my only friend. I'm scared I'll go to prison if Dylan finds out. Oh, what am I going to DO?'

I could only be with her, and kiss her face, and purr, but the autumn days raced on and nothing happened. Until today.

The heavy footsteps woke me up and I saw a pair of swollen, purple legs coming through the gate, and another set of legs in black boots and jeans. Dylan!

His mum was a mountain of a woman, her aura fizzling with indignation as she waddled down the path with Dylan slouching behind her, his eyes downcast. She didn't use the doorbell, but banged the door with her fist.

Amber barked and barked, but she knocked again. 'I ain't scared of your bloody dog. Come on, answer. I ain't going nowhere 'til you've 'eard what I got to say.' She sniffed loudly.

Alarmed, I ran, low to the ground, round the side of the house to the kitchen door, through the cat flap and under the sofa where I felt safe.

Max was getting up out of his armchair.

'Who on earth is that? Stop barking, Amber.'

Amber ran to his side, her hackles ridged along her back. Max took her by the collar, dragged her into the conservatory and shut the door. 'QUIET. On your bed, now.'

He opened the front door, and Dylan's mum came billowing into the hall.

'Excuse me ... I don't recall inviting you in,' protested Max, but his voice just blew away through the open door like a discarded leaf. Ignoring him, she barged into the lounge, with Dylan following, looking lost and sullen in her intimidating presence.

There was no place to hide. Diana was lying on the sofa with a blue blanket over her, and TammyLee was sitting in the chair beside her, engrossed in playing with her mobile.

'Is that 'er?' Dylan's mum asked him, jerking her thumb at TammyLee.

'Yeah.'

'Right, you ... you got some explaining to do, my girl.' Dylan's mum folded her fat arms. 'And I ain't leaving 'til you come clean about what YOU did with MY grandchild.'

TammyLee couldn't seem to find words to reply.

In the shocked silence that followed, the house was filled with the roar of heavy rain. Max stood up and assembled the shreds of his authority.

'And you are?' he asked acidly.

''Is mum.' She jerked a thumb at Dylan, who was shuffling from one foot to the other. 'Iris Fredrickson.'

'Well now, Iris Fredrickson ... what gives you the right to barge into our home, un-invited? Especially with this ... this boy in tow. He's not welcome here, and neither are you. So kindly leave.'

'I don't take no notice of the likes of you,' Iris said, looking contemptuously at Max. 'Think you're so bloody good, don't you? Well, your daughter is a lying whore.'

TammyLee leaped to her feet.

'I AM NOT,' she hissed. 'You don't even know me.'

'Don't want to, either.'

'You've no idea who I am or what kind of life I have,' TammyLee said. 'You only know what Dylan's told you. He feels guilty about dropping my cat in the river ... animal cruelty that was... I could have reported him for it ... so he's just winding you up with stuff he's fabricating to get attention. That's what he is, an attention seeker. Everyone knows that.'

'Now you listen to me, my girl.' Iris moved closer and jabbed a fat finger at TammyLee's face.

'No, you listen.' TammyLee stamped her foot, and even from under the sofa, I could feel the heat of her anger. I wished I was a tiger that could leap out and defend her. 'I don't have a life like most girls my age. I come home from college and care for my mum,' she said, waving a hand at Diana, who was calmly watching.

'That don't make you a saint,' said Iris.

'WHAT is this about?' demanded Max. 'Will someone please tell me?' He looked searchingly from one to the other, while torrents of rain lashed at the windows. It was nearly dark outside, but inside the fire flickered orange, and there was light that only I could see. It was the shine of angels who were mostly around Diana.

I chose that moment to emerge from under the sofa. I had to help. With my tail up and eyes bright, I was aware of the empowering light as I stood there bravely, a very small cat in the midst of angry, towering humans. Who should I go to? I wanted to be with Diana, or TammyLee – that would have been the obvious choice. But I looked at Iris, first. I'd seen her swollen legs coming through the gate and her fist thumping the door. Now I looked for her eyes, which were embedded in the folds of an unhappy face. I examined her aura and it was in tatters. Her heart was tightly wrapped in layers of misery.

She looked down at me looking up at her and melted. That's when I knew exactly what to do. I targeted her, brushing my waving tail around those swollen legs as I glided to and fro. I stood up on my back legs, purring, and dabbed at her skirt with paws of velvet.

Everyone was watching me.

Iris couldn't resist me. She reached down and smoothed me, and it was obvious from her touch that she loved cats. Without asking permission, she picked me up and I let her. I made a fuss of her, purring, and gazing into her eyes.

'You don't have to be angry,' I was telling her, by telepathy. 'You can talk quietly, like Diana, and then the angels will help you.' I talked directly to her soul. It shone like a lamp in the distance, and as she responded to my love – it came closer and she began to relax.

Diana decided to help me. 'Well,' she said. 'Tallulah loves you, doesn't she? Now, why don't you sit down in that armchair, with Tallulah? And Dylan, you sit there, on the stool by the fire ... you look cold, poor lad. And let's talk this over, quietly, and calmly, shall we?'

Diana would have made a good cat, I thought approvingly. She was so lovely, and quietly spoken, no one could get mad with her. I saw Dylan glance at her with disbelief and longing in his eyes.

'You sit here, love. I'll move my feet,' she said to TammyLee, who was staring at me with an incredulous expression.

Everyone sat down exactly where Diana had told them to, and I began work on Iris's heart. Only Max was still standing, looking bewildered as he often did when faced with the radiance of Diana's love. She looked at him. 'Now why don't you go and get those sandbags, Max? Listen to that rain.' She turned to Iris and spoke to her as if she was a long-lost friend. 'We have to be so careful living close to the river.'

'Absolutely not,' said Max. 'I'm staying right here until this is sorted out.'

His voice sounded raucous in the quiet atmosphere Diana and I had created. Dylan sat mutinously on the stool, studying the flames leaping up the chimney. I noticed a handbag dangling from one of Iris's arms. 'Just wait until you put that down,' I thought. 'I'll have that open in seconds and see what's inside.'

But Iris opened the handbag first, and

took out a folded piece of newspaper. She hung the bag back on her arm.

'THAT's what this is about.' She unfolded the paper and thrust it at Max. 'And don't even think about tearing it up. I got copies.'

Max frowned as he read what was on the paper, and handed it to Diana.

'Oh, yes, I remember that poor little baby,' Diana said. 'I hope someone nice adopted him and I hope the mum is all right. She must have been desperate to abandon her baby.'

'I don't call it desperate. EVIL, that's what I call it,' said Iris loudly. She pointed at TammyLee. 'SHE's the mother. Ask her, go on ... ask her.'

Her accusation rang around the room. Even Diana looked shocked. TammyLee put her head in her hands.

'There you are. Look at 'er. Guilty!' Iris announced triumphantly.

'That's an appalling accusation,' said Max. 'Can you substantiate it?'

'SHE can.' Iris pointed at TammyLee.

'Don't be ridiculous,' said Max. He looked at TammyLee. 'It's not true, is it? Tell me it's not true.'

Diana put both arms round TammyLee and held her tightly. 'Surely this isn't true, darling? Darling?' TammyLee was silent, holding the edges of her secret together with a long practised strength.

Iris was using up my love so fast I didn't think I could give any more. I jumped down and ran to the sofa, to sit between Tammy-Lee and Diana, and from there I could see Amber's puzzled face watching us through the glass door, her tail down.

The talking went on, and on, with the clock ticking loudly in the silence and the rain adding a hush to the house. The flames in the fireplace lost their energy and began to glow, and sink into scarlet.

Seeming to be intimidated by his mum, Dylan took no part in the conversation, only responding with a grunt or a shrug. They argued about dates and lies, while Diana sat with the newspaper picture of Rocky in her hands, smoothing it and gazing at the baby's bright little face.

After one of the silences, she said, 'So ... you think that this little boy is my grandson?'

'And mine,' said Iris. She pointed at TammyLee. 'And she's the mother. Aren't you? Come on, admit it.'

'I'm not admitting anything,' said Tammy-Lee stonily.

Iris leaned forward in her chair. 'Then if you won't admit it, we'll have no choice. I'm not letting this go. We'll go to the social workers ... and my son will have a DNA test done. At least he's coming clean about what he did ... and he wants to be a father to that baby. You lot think my Dylan's a bad boy, but I know different. If he's got the guts to own up, why haven't you ... Tammy whatever your name is? Stubborn aren't you? ... Madam!'

'Will you SHUT UP!' screamed Tammy-Lee, her hands clutching her temples. 'Just shut the hell up and get out of our house. GO. Just GO.'

'Please, darling ... shh ... it's OK. Max and I will support you whatever happens ... we're here.' Diana turned to Iris. 'I think ... it would be best if you go and leave us to talk to our Tam on her own. Then we'll get back to you, I promise. Can you understand that ... as a mum?'

'She's right,' said Max.

Iris folded her arms and sat back. 'I ain't moving 'til she admits it,' she said. 'Get the police if you like ... they'll be interested in what I've got to say. I ain't moving.'

Dylan rolled his eyes and tried to intervene.

'Mum! We can't stay here all night. I want

to get home.'

She shot him down. 'Don't you start. Don't you dare tell me what to do!'

Max walked across to the window and looked out. 'It's raining, pouring,' he said, 'and in view of our proximity to the river, which is already full to the brim, I think you should go and I'm going to drive you home. Otherwise, you'll end up sleeping here with no electricity. And before you object to that, I would point out that it's a generous offer ... kind of me, considering the way you barged in here, uninvited.'

'Tomorrow's another day,' said Diana. 'We need time to sort this out, Iris. It's a shock, yes, but IF it's true, these two young people will need our support, not condemnation. I'm concerned for my daughter, and I'm sure you are for Dylan. We shouldn't involve the police at all. It's a family matter.'

'Thanks.' Dylan looked at Diana as if she was rescuing him. 'I'm not a bad person like you think... I ... I'm sorry for what I did to the cat ... it was stupid ... peer pressure and stuff.'

'Yeah, and drugs,' said TammyLee.

'I'm off it. I'm clean now.'

''E is,' said Iris, 'without any help from the medics.'

'Pigs might fly,' TammyLee muttered.

'This isn't going anywhere,' said Max, taking his raincoat from its peg and jingling his car keys. 'I'm going now so make your minds up.'

Dylan stood up. 'Look, Mum,' he said, putting his face close to hers, 'you know you can't walk home in this rain, and there won't be a bus for hours. Have some sense. This isn't the last day in the history of the universe.'

Iris sighed. She glowered at TammyLee, and handed her a slip of paper. 'That's my mobile number and, if I haven't got the truth from you by tomorrow, I'll be back ... with the socials.' She unzipped her handbag, extracted a voluminous pink raincoat from a pouch and put it on with much rustling.

As soon as they had gone, TammyLee let Amber out of the conservatory, and we listened to the rain pounding the glass roof, and the splashing of Max's car driving off into the night.

Diana and TammyLee stayed on the sofa, not speaking, but TammyLee wouldn't look at her mum. I returned to the warm hearth rug with Amber and began to wash vigorously, feeling I needed to cleanse my coat of the last traces of the hostility Iris had

213

generated in our home.

Diana was holding TammyLee's hand, and gazing expectantly at her. If she'd kept quiet, it might have been OK, but, in her softest voice, she asked that same painful question: 'Is it true?'

TammyLee looked at her, desperately and wordlessly. Then she lurched to her feet and stumbled out of the room and up the stairs. Minutes later she hurried down again, clad in high boots, a black parka and with her hair stuffed into the hood, which was falling forward over her face.

I heard Diana gasp as her daughter fled past and flung the front door open. The wind blasted hard raindrops and yellow leaves into the hall. TammyLee slammed the door behind her, and we heard her footsteps vanishing into the night.

I jumped onto the windowsill and ducked under the curtain to see which way she was going, and I saw her hooded silhouette, a bag flying from her shoulder. She headed down the road towards the busy roundabout where the headlights lit up the driving rain and the water pouring down both sides of the road.

I was used to TammyLee coming and going, so her flight from the house didn't bother me. But it worried Diana.

I'd never seen her so upset. She sat with her eyes shut and her hands clinging to a patchwork cushion that TammyLee had made, repeating over and over again, 'Oh, God, please look after our Tam. Let her come back, please.'

Even the solid presence of Amber leaning against her legs didn't seem to help. I went on washing and grooming my fur until it felt silky and clean. Then I looked round for something to play with. After all the rage and the rows the humans imposed on me, I needed time to be a cat.

I padded around, sniffing the places where Dylan and Iris had sat, and made an amazing discovery. Iris had left her handbag behind! Wow. I circled it a few times, eyeing the worn leather toggle on the zip, patted it, and did my pouncing routine, leaping and twizzling in the air. I crouched and sidled, never taking my eyes from the zip toggle in case it moved, loving the excitement and fun building inside me.

Little beads of joy raced through my heart. With delicate skill, I got the toggle between my teeth, held the bag down with my paws, and pulled. It slid open with a satisfying buzz. Now I could see inside. I did my pounce routine again, then reached my paw into the soft interior and extracted an open roll of peppermints. The smell of them, and the spiral of torn green wrapping, freaked me out and I chased it towards Amber. She sniffed at it and stuck her nose high in the air. 'I'm not allowed to have those,' she said, but I left them there for her, and returned to the open bag.

Next, I took out a bunch of keys, which smelled awful. Attached to them was a tiny lion with a fuzzy mane and eyes that rolled around comically. He wasn't brilliant to play with because I couldn't detach him from the keys. I went on burrowing, and extracted a rattly packet of tablets in silver foil, and a biscuit wrapped in cellophane. I was just hooking out the purse, when Amber started barking and Max came back in.

'Iris left her handbag behind,' he said, rolling his eyes. 'And I see you've been busy, Tallulah!' Tutting, he scooped up the stuff I'd taken out and put it back, but no one laughed, and that was unusual. This time, my attempt to break up the misery with a bit of humour was not appreciated.

'Back soon,' said Max. 'I'll pick up some sandbags.'

'No ... Max ... wait,' cried Diana, her face taut with anxiety.

216

'What is it, love?' In two strides, Max was beside her, looking concerned. But Diana couldn't seem to speak. She clutched his arm and took some deep breaths.

'Our Tam has run away,' she sobbed. 'Never mind the sandbags ... you've got to find her, Max ... she's so vulnerable just now ... and she ran out the door in black clothes. She'll get hit by a car. Oh, please, please look for her, Max ... she might do something terrible, the state she's in.'

'Silly girl,' said Max. 'What about you, here on your own?'

'I'll be OK for a few hours,' wept Diana. 'Please, just go and look for her. And don't shout at her, Max, please. She's very, very emotionally fragile right now.'

Chapter Thirteen

THE LION IN WINTER

Hours later, Max came back, without TammyLee.

'No sign of her,' he said. 'I checked all the usual places where she goes. Her mobile is turned off. If she's not back in the morning, we'll report her missing.'

The anxiety stretched itself into every corner of the house. Max made up the fire and brewed cocoa in silence. He washed up and fed Amber, and put some fresh cat litter in my tray. 'Don't you go out, Tallulah,' he said. Amber was allowed out, and came back with her legs dripping wet. Then Max lit candles and stood them in the window in jars. He persuaded Diana to go upstairs to bed. 'While you can,' he said. 'If the power goes off, you won't have the stair lift.'

'I can't possibly sleep,' said Diana, 'not while my TammyLee is out there. I don't want my medication tonight, Max... I need to stay awake.'

Max stayed up with her and we heard their voices talking. Amber and I had had enough of the stress. We needed a long sleep, and we needed each other. I was glad to lie on the hearth rug with her, even though she was snoring and having one of her woofy dreams. The rhythm of her breath, and the purr of the fire, was comforting. The sound of the rain seemed distant, but the night was full of unfamiliar swishing and gurgling sounds.

Later, I was wide awake for a while and I trotted upstairs to TammyLee's room, to see if she was there, and she wasn't. I rolled about on the duvet and played with the soft edge of it. Then I jumped onto the shelf of teddy bears and walked along it with my tail up, inspecting them. They hadn't got auras, only the twinkling eyes gave them a presence, and their black noses and stitched-on smiles. Next, I sat on TammyLee's laptop, to think. I sat on her chair, and on her pillow. Where was she? I wanted her.

What if she never came back? Whose cat would I be then?

'Worrying won't help you,' said my angel. 'The next three days are what you need to focus on, and you must look after YOUR-SELF, Tallulah. You are a very important cat, and you are so loved ... we need you to survive.'

'Survive what?' I asked, but my angel disappeared in a shimmy of light, and I was left alone on TammyLee's bed. Survive? What, again?

There was silence from Diana's room, so I ran downstairs to Amber and snuggled up to her. She sighed and put a warm paw over me, as if she wanted to hug me. I purred a little and went to sleep between her big paws, knowing that if I heard TammyLee's footsteps, I'd be instantly awake, and so would Amber.

The candles flickered until dawn, and the sunrise was silver grey. Drops of rain still covered the windows and there was an unfamiliar light outside, and no sounds of traffic, which was unusual. A loud metallic throbbing sound filled the air, coming and going as if some great machine was patrolling the sky.

Amber seemed tense. She wouldn't talk to me, but stood in the doorway, listening, her tail down. I was OK, refreshed from my sleep and wanting to go out in the garden. Heading for the cat flap, I ran through the kitchen with my tail up, hoping TammyLee would be on her way back. The kitchen floor was wet, causing me to stop and shake each paw. I butted my head against the cat flap and jumped out. Too late, I saw water shining, directly outside, and there was no avoiding it. The whole garden shone like a lake. Even the path was submerged and water was lapping at the walls of the house. With my paws and tummy horribly wet and cold, I turned and went back through the cat flap. The hearth rug was still warm, and Amber came to me, whining, and tried to lick me dry. She was comforting, but I wanted TammyLee to come and fluff me up with a towel. I needed her there, to cuddle me and explain what was happening. I missed her kindness.

Amber ran to the window and put her paws up on the sill, looking out as if someone was coming. I leaped up there, and stared, transfixed by what was happening outside. Max had stacked sandbags across the gate, and a line of gleaming muddy brown water was spilling over the top of them. Out in the road, the water was flowing along like a river, and, in the distance, voices were shouting. The sky throbbed with circling helicopters.

A duck with a green head lurched over the top of the sandbags and started swimming around our garden as if it owned the place. I sat up very straight and batted the window, trying to tell that duck exactly what I would do to it if I was out there.

Amber was watching, but her tail wasn't wagging and her eyes looked worried. Then she did something that seriously spooked me. She lifted her head, stretched her throat, and howled, on and on. It chilled me to my bones. It resounded through the house, along the floor and up the walls, into corners and cupboards, even the lamp-shades quivered with it.

My fur ruffed out, my eyes must have gone black with terror, and my pulse raced. But

Amber didn't stop. The howling went on and on, like a warning siren.

Too petrified to move, I watched the water in the garden. I saw Max's sandbag wall sag and burst open, and a torrent of brown water surged towards the house with an unforgettable roar. It burst through the cat flap in a plume of froth, swept across the kitchen and into the hall.

Amber stopped howling and barked. She spun round and lolloped through the water and up the stairs, leaving me paralysed with terror on the windowsill.

I watched in horror as my food bowl, still with some bits in it, floated by, along with the leaves and litter the water was bringing in. I watched the brown tide, foaming at the edges, glide into the lounge and under the sofa, swirling around the chair legs, soaking the carpet. It picked up TammyLee's fluffy slippers and sloshed them against the wall. Then it reached the fireplace and steam rose, hissing from the embers.

'What the hell is the matter with that dog?'

I heard Max getting up, his feet creaking across the landing.

'Oh, my GOD. Now we have got problems.'

He dived into the bedroom and grabbed a

mobile phone, tapping it urgently and listening.

'Damn it. The lines are jammed.' He did a lot of cursing, and finally spoke to someone. 'Our house is flooded. The water's pouring in, and my wife is disabled ... and my teenage daughter has gone missing.'

He didn't say, 'Our cat is marooned on the windowsill.' I was, and the water was creeping up the wall, deeper and deeper. I clung there, watching Max, who was now downstairs and paddling around, grabbing armfuls of stuff and chucking it on the stairs. I was afraid that in his frenzy, he wouldn't notice me, so I meowed loudly; in fact, I wailed. He waded over and picked me up. Phew!

'Poor Tallulah,' he said as I clung to his shoulder. He carried me to the stairs and put me on them. 'Go upstairs, go on. Shoo!' He clapped his hands which wasn't helpful to an already frightened cat.

Miffed, I crouched on the top step, watching Amber, who was trying to convince Max it was a game. She was charging up and down what was left of the stairs, grabbing some of the things he was chucking up there, and carrying them into Diana's room in her mouth. She grabbed books, papers, shoes and gadgets, even a telephone with its wires trailing. She got that tangled up in the banister rail, and tugged at it until Max shouted at her. She left it swinging in mid-air and seized a coat by its hood, dragging it round the corner into Diana's room.

An amazing sound rippled through the house. Diana was laughing! It relaxed me straight away and I ran in to see her with my tail up. What Amber had done was awesome, in my opinion. In the midst of a crisis, she'd managed to make Diana laugh. It made me feel better.

But it had the opposite effect on Max.

'What the hell is there to laugh at?' He shouted. 'I'm busting a gut trying to salvage our belongings. What's so funny?'

His words only sent Diana into a new bout of hysterical giggling, and encouraged Amber to move even faster, her tail wagging now, knocking medicine bottles off tables as she flew past.

'I'm sorry, love,' said Diana as Max's furious face appeared at the door. 'I know I shouldn't be laughing but Amber is so funny ... don't be cross with her, Max. It's better to laugh than cry.'

'I'll do the crying,' said Max. 'Our home is RUINED, Diana. Our daughter is missing. For God's sake, woman.'

He did start to cry, sitting at the top of the stairs, but he refused to let the tears flow. Silently and painfully, he fought it, his shoulders shuddering with every breath. I ran to him and looked right into his soul with my most concerned cat stare.

'Tallulah ... you lovely, lovely cat,' he said, and caressed my fur with an unsteady hand. 'What are we going to do with you and Amber? And, dear God, where IS my daughter?'

Max shut Amber and me in TammyLee's bedroom, with a dish of water. Amber lay down across the door with a sigh of resignation, and I made a nest in the duvet and fell into a restorative sleep.

It must have been mid-afternoon when the house began to shake. Amber was frightened of thunderstorms, and she crawled under the table and pressed herself against the wall, whimpering. It wasn't thunder, I knew that. Keeping myself hidden behind the curtain, I peeped out, alarmed to see a helicopter hovering just above the house. My ears hurt with the bang-banging of its relentless blades, and, up close, the helicopter was enormous, deafening and intimidating.

My instinct was to hide like Amber, but I

wanted to see what was happening. It felt as if the house was going to be blown to bits. I touched the window with my nose, and the glass was vibrating.

The sky was blue now and the flood had settled into a vast sheet of water. I could see the reflection of the helicopter and the trees. Loud and scary as it was, I worked out that this iron giant was actually under control. In the midst of the thunderous noise, there were voices, and they were calm, giving clear instructions to each other. I understood that a man in goggles and a helmet was in the cockpit, and he was OK. Two more men, clad in bright orange, were in the side door, and one of them began to descend, on a string, like a spider!

Down and down he came, and stopped level with Diana's bedroom window. Max was holding on to her tightly, and Diana was being brave, smiling and making jokes as the man fixed a harness round her. She was whisked up into the sky, with the man in orange holding her firmly. She looked down at me as I sat in the window, and then she was lifted into the helicopter. Max went next, his body rigid, his face grim as he was winched to safety.

'What about us?' I thought, expecting the

men in orange to come back with a cat cage and lift me up there too, and Amber, and take us to a lovely place where TammyLee would be waiting. I wanted her so much in that moment. I wanted her love, and the special way she talked to me and explained things, the way she'd put her face close to mine and call me 'magic puss cat'.

But it didn't happen like that. A cold shadow of betrayal crept over me as they closed the door of the rescue helicopter. I meowed and scrabbled at the window. I wailed and cried, but the helicopter rose heartlessly into the sky and set off at speed, carrying Max and Diana away from us. I watched until it was a tiny speck against the western sky.

They had left us behind.

Max's words rang in my head. 'Our home is RUINED.' What did he mean? It seemed OK to me, except that there was water down-stairs. I wondered where my food dish was.

Amber crawled out from under the table, still shivering. I tried to comfort her by winding myself round her legs with my tail brushing her face, but all it did was make her sneeze. My attempt to tell her about the helicopter was a waste of time. She couldn't get her head round it. She stood at the door, pawing it and whining, her tail hanging limp like rope. Her fur had mostly dried except for her ears, and she was cold, and, like me, hungry.

Outside, the sun was setting and pink light reflected in the water. Amber wouldn't talk to me, so I sat in the window and watched it getting dark. Boats were going up the flooded road, laden with people wrapped in blankets. One woman had a cat in a cage and I could hear it meowing. The other cat I saw was all alone and clinging to a wooden table that was being swept along fast by the surging water. I searched the sky, but the helicopter didn't come back, and in the deepening twilight there were blue lights flashing everywhere.

It was the longest night of my life, thinking I'd been abandoned, wanting TammyLee, wanting my supper and the warm bright fire. Amber didn't sleep either but stared at the door all night, her nose twitching, and her tail didn't wag once.

When dawn came, I noticed her looking up at the door handle and getting more and more agitated. She seemed to be hyping herself up for something she was planning to do. Then, cleverly, she got the handle between her teeth and pushed it down. It didn't work, but she tried again, and I ran to sit beside her and encourage her, thinking we could get down to the kitchen and find our food. Amber growled and jerked the handle harder, and at last the door swung open. Amber dashed into Diana's room, and came out again, looking puzzled. She ran up and down the landing and in and out of the bathroom.

'Max and Diana are gone,' I said, 'and TammyLee.'

'I don't believe you,' said Amber. 'They're out there somewhere.'

She sat at the top of the stairs, sniffing the air and thinking.

'Don't go down there,' I said. 'It's flooded.'

The water was deep. Stuff was floating around in it, and only the top of the sofa and table were visible. Sticks and straw had been washed in and was drifting around with lots of paper and plastic bottles. We could see into the kitchen, and the window was open, and once Amber saw that, something even more terrible happened.

'Don't go ... please,' I begged, but Amber wasn't seeing or hearing me.

With a sense of foreboding, I watched her pad down the stairs. She entered the water quietly, not with her usual joyful splash. She swam around in a circle, and looked up at me, and clearly she was saying, 'Goodbye.'

Devastated, I meowed and meowed, but Amber swam into the kitchen, and dragged herself over the worktop and out of the open window. Frantic, I tore back into Tammy-Lee's room, to see what happened, and glimpsed the shine of Amber's wet head as she swam across the flooded garden and into the swirling current that was the road. I meowed my loudest. What chance did a lone dog have in that vast and swiftly moving flood?

Now I was truly alone.

I spent most of the morning meowing, going from one window to another, hoping to see someone who would notice me. Nobody was out there now – even the boats had gone, and the helicopters were far away. I clung to a frail idea that Amber might come back, and I worried about my family. TammyLee was the one I ached to see.

Clouds gathered over the midday sun and soon it was raining again. Mist hung over the water, and the place looked desolate. The day was passing and I hadn't been rescued. Starving hungry, I ate some bread and cheese Max had left, but it upset me and I was sick. I missed being in the garden and thought that going outside would make me feel better.

'You must help yourself,' said my angel, and I flicked my tail in annoyance. But last time she'd said that, it had worked. I sat in the front window, thinking, studying the flooded landscape for escape routes, wondering if it might be possible to go along the tops of fences and trees. First I had to find a way out of the house. Swimming was not an option. Meowing at boats hadn't worked. I studied parts of the roof visible from the window and noticed a skylight that was open just a crack.

I found it in the bathroom. The crack was too small, but if I got my paws up there and pushed, I could squeeze out. Jumping up was a challenge, especially from the floor. I clambered onto the shiny lid of the loo, then onto the cistern, and from this narrow slippery perch, I planned my daring leap. I had to try. Focusing on the power in my back legs, and the sharpness of my claws, I sprang up there. For a frantic moment, I hung with my claws dug into the wood. With all my strength, I lifted my hind legs, butted the crack with my head, and wriggled through. I was out!

It had stopped raining, so I walked up to the ridge of the roof to survey the landscape. Somewhere an engine was running, and I soon discovered it was a fire engine, sucking water out of a nearby house. I sat on the roof and meowed, but no one even looked in my direction, and my cries for help were lost in the noise of the fire engine.

I was hungry, and thirsty, and cold.

Night came with frightening speed. Another night of being abandoned, this time on my own. Thinking the roof was not a good place to spend the night, I went back to the open skylight, intending to attempt the jump back into the bathroom. But I made a dreadful mistake by putting my weight on the raised edge of the window and making it shut. My entrance was closed, and despite my efforts to reopen it, it stayed closed.

With thick darkness and a chilly wind blowing, there was no choice but to spend the night on the roof, with no soft place to sleep, no food, no water, and no one to love me.

Chapter Fourteen

CATS IN CAGES

I pressed myself against the chimney on its warmest side. Cold and isolated up on the roof, I tried to conserve my energy by tucking my paws under my body and dozing quietly. Staying calm was vital to my survival. No more meowing.

It ought to have been peaceful, but suddenly the roof tiles were vibrating, first from a loud clanking noise, followed by a steady rhythmic pounding, like footsteps. I could feel my eyes growing big with fright. Was the roof somehow trying to shake me off into the water?

The rhythmic pounding stopped, and, in the expectant pause, I sensed a listening, and a beam of light came sweeping over the roof. Then, an unbelievable sound.

Someone was calling, 'Kitty kitty kitty.'

A gentle, male voice, up there on the roof. It wasn't anyone I knew, but from past experience, I assumed that 'kitty kitty kitty', meant me.

Someone had found me!

I peeped round the chimney and the light dazzled me. Whoever was holding it turned it off, and I stared down at a fireman in a helmet, his face looking up at me. He looked solid and reassuring, obviously a cat lover.

My tail shot up, and my fur bushed out with joy. I couldn't get to him fast enough. I slithered down the wet tiles, doing purr-meows in gratitude. A friend, a warm, human friend. It was so comforting to lean against his chest and hear the slow heartbeat. I clung to his shoulder, and cried like a little kitten.

'You're a beauty!' he said, appreciatively. 'You're gorgeous. Now you hang on to me and I'll take you down. Trust me. OK?'

How could I not trust this cuddly fireman? I hung on, and treated him to my loudest purr as he took me carefully down the ladder. It didn't even bother me when he put me in a cat cage. I was being rescued!

The fireman waded a long way through the flood to a patch of higher ground. A fire engine was parked there, its blue light flickering, reflected in the water. Behind it was a van with a familiar figure waiting at the wheel.

'Got her. She's fine,' the fireman shouted.

'Can you take her?'

'I've just got room, my luvvy. Thank you SO much. You're a star.'

She took the cage from the fireman, and looked in at me. 'Tallulah! Hello, my luvvy. It's me, Penny, the cat lady. Now don't you worry, we'll take care of you and find your people.'

I was a lucky cat, and if I'd been a human, I'd have given Penny a box of Cadbury's Roses like the one Max had given Tammy-Lee for passing her exams.

The interior of the van was full of cat cages, and there was a cacophony of meowing and yowling. Black frightened eyes looked out, and most of the cats were extremely upset. I did a lot of work in the back of that van, showing them how to be calm and telling them about the work of Cats Protection. As Penny drove up the hill away from the flood, those traumatised cats were looking at me, their eyes hungry for reassurance. The worst was a Siamese with blue tormented eyes and the loudest voice I'd ever heard from a cat.

'You're upsetting everyone,' I said, 'and it's no good wasting your energy on meowing. It won't make any difference. Penny is a good and clever human. She'll find your people for you.'

But the Siamese cat ignored me.

I thought Penny would take us to the farm with the cat pens, but she didn't. When she pulled into a car park and turned off the engine, the yowling and meowing made eerie music ring through the night.

Where were we?

She opened the back door and outside was a big building like a school, with the lights on and people milling about inside. I wished I could read the tall red words on a board outside. Penny picked up my curiosity immediately and read them for me:

'FLOOD DISASTER CENTRE.'

I could smell soup and bacon, and hear teacups clattering. From another part of the building came the smell of wet dogs, and the sound of barking. I listened for the particular bark I longed to hear... Amber! ... but no, she wasn't there, I was certain.

'Is Amber in the spirit world?' I asked my angel, fearing that her answer would be 'yes'.

'No,' she said, 'not yet.'

'Then where is she?'

'She is lost.'

I thought of my wonderful dog being lost out there in the flooded landscape, and sent her a message: 'Stay where you are, Amber, these kind people will find you.' Somewhere she was shivering and alone, like I had been on the roof. I hoped the power of my thoughts would help her not to give up.

A group of smiling 'cat ladies' came to the back of the van and carried our cat cages in a meowing procession in through brightly lit glass doors, and down a corridor. I was proud that Penny, the Queen of Cat Ladies had chosen ME to carry.

The building was warm and full of noise. People talking and children screaming and running about. We passed the kitchen and I sniffed the aromatic steam rising from massive cauldrons and trays of food. Beef, chicken and herby smells. I was absolutely starving.

'Trust you to know where the kitchen is, Tallulah,' said Penny when I meowed. 'Don't worry, you'll get one of my nice sachets of rabbit in a minute.'

They took us into a shiny room with a high ceiling. It was full of bewildered cats, all in cages around the walls. Some were sitting, hunched up and staring miserably out. Others were cowering in the back of their cage, or weaving to and fro, trying hopelessly to escape. I wished the people would open the cages and let me sit in the middle and gather them round me for a communal purring session.

The promised sachet of rabbit arrived, and Penny popped it into my cage on a plastic dish. Nothing had ever tasted so scrumptious. I ate every bit, and cleaned the dish with my tongue. I sat calmly, washing, and waiting to see what would happen. The door opened, and an elderly man came in, his eyes searching the cat cages, and the Siamese cat yelled out at him. He stumbled across the room with tears glistening on his cheeks.

'Judy! My Judy!'

He opened the cage and the Siamese cat's blue eyes sparkled. She could talk, almost like a human, and the love radiated from her aura as she climbed into his arms, kissing his face and hugging him with her long paws. Then she dived inside his coat and nestled in there, her eyes half closed and blissful as she looked out at the rest of us.

Through the evening there were more emotional reunions as people turned up to find their lost cats. It was a happy time, but not for me. My confidence was draining away. Every time the door opened, a tiny flame of hope started in my heart, and quickly died when I saw yet another sad and frightened cat being joyfully reclaimed, and it wasn't me. I was tired, and the unfamiliar comings and goings resounded through the building. The effort of listening for a voice I knew was intense. Even Penny disappeared and a different cat lady took her place, but she didn't know me. I was just another cat.

My eyes began to close. It didn't feel right to be in that harshly lit noisy place late at night when I would normally have been curled up on TammyLee's bed. The children's voices changed from happy playing to screaming and crying, along with the raised voices of exasperated mothers trying to get them to sleep. Plates and pans were being crashed around in the kitchen, doors were banging, and people were shouting to each other. My head ached and my ears hurt with the noise. Sleep was impossible.

I did doze a bit and dreamed I heard Amber barking, waking me up with a jump that shook my whole body. The noise went on all night, and the lights stayed painfully bright. I only knew it was morning when the windows turned silver, and a wild wind swirled leaves across the car park.

The new cat lady brought me a meal but I was now so stressed and exhausted I didn't touch it. My joy at being rescued was fast turning into despair, and I needed a litter tray. I couldn't stay in that cage much longer!

And then ... I heard running feet. Clonk, clonk across the car park. A figure in black, with flying hair, ran past the window. I sat up, my heart beating fast, my neck getting longer as I watched the door. And hope came flooding into my tired mind like sacred sunlight. Suddenly, I was warm, and alive, and alert.

I listened.

The footsteps I knew and loved! In the building now, marching along the shiny corridor, closer, and closer. And then my heart leaped with excitement. Another set of footsteps was running alongside, the click-click of a dog's nails on the hard floor, and when they stopped, there was the thump-thump of a tail wagging against the wall. The cat lady stood up and went to the door.

She opened it and peeked out. An argument started.

'I am afraid you can't bring that dog in here.'

'But she is OK with cats.'

'I am sure she is, dear, but I have got a room full of traumatised cats, and the last thing they need is a dog.'

'But my cat is friends with her.'

'Yes, but the other cats aren't. They've been rescued from the floods ... one was even found clinging to a bit of wood in the river. I am sorry, but you CANNOT bring a dog in. There's a place for dogs at the other end of the building.'

I heard a sigh.

'I've been through hell to get here. I waded through the floods and stuff, and I need to see if my cat is here. I'm not going away. Look, I'm dripping wet and freezing.'

'All right, dear, don't get upset. I'll hold the dog, and you go in ... but please, DO NOT let any of those cats out, even yours.'

'Thanks. I won't.'

The door opened. I fluffed my fur, and sat up, determined to look beautiful. Then I heard a whisper that filled the room, and all the cats went quiet. 'Where are you, Magic puss cat?'

I meowed my loudest and my TammyLee turned her head and saw me. 'Tallulah!' she cried, and ran across the room to me, and undid the cage door immediately, her bangles jingling as she reached in and picked me up with ice-cold hands. My whole body turned into a purring machine as TammyLee lifted me into her arms. She smelled of the river, and her hair was wet, but I didn't care. We loved each other. I wrapped myself round her neck, my warm fur drying her like a soft towel, the way she had so often dried me. She kissed my face and I kept butting my head into hers, giving her every last spark of my love.

'Magic puss cat,' she sobbed, and the tears were happy tears. 'I thought I'd lost you for ever. Darling cat. I'm sorry I ran out on you. Please forgive me, Tallulah.'

Forgive her? Of course I did. It's what cats do. I turned my purring up a notch, and let it tickle her ear until she giggled.

My angel was whirling round and round us, enjoying herself, whisking ribbons of stars through TammyLee's aura.

'I'd better pop you back in, Tallulah,' she said after our long cuddle. 'But I won't leave you. I don't know where we'll end up going, but you are staying with me.'

I didn't mind being back in the cage because TammyLee was carrying it, and this time it was my turn to look blissfully triumphant with the other cats watching enviously.

'And guess who's outside,' TammyLee said, as we headed towards the door.

I'd already guessed. Amber!

Like TammyLee, she was soaking wet, but so pleased to see me. The cat lady let go of her lead and Amber was so excited that she tried to gallop in small circles on the slippery floor. Then she sneezed right into my cage and her tail sent the cat lady's papers flying from the chair. But she managed to make them both laugh. I envied her that talent.

'Behave, Amber. SIT,' said TammyLee sternly and Amber did sit down, facing me, and I noticed she was shivering.

'She swam all the way from the park,' said TammyLee. 'And I didn't find her ... she found me and she actually stopped me going into the river! She's such a clever dog. But look at her ... she's really cold.'

'Take her down there ... to the RSPCA dog-rescue room. They've got hairdryers and towels and loads of food. People have been donating stuff,' said the cat lady. 'They'll sort her out, poor girlie. Here, I'll take her down. You go and find your family.'

'Mum's in hospital,' said TammyLee, 'and Dad's with her. They're OK, but mum's got MS, so she needs some help.'

'And so do you. Go on, you go to the main centre, they're doing breakfast for about two hundred people.'

She gave TammyLee a cat harness and a lead. 'If you want to let the cat out, put this on her and keep her attached to you. She might panic in that noisy place.'

All I wanted to do was sleep. I felt safe now, with TammyLee, and Amber, and I trusted that we would eventually go home. So I switched off and slept while TammyLee sat at a table and ate breakfast. I must have slept for hours, for when I woke up, we were in a different room, and Amber was there, lying on TammyLee's feet. She looked dry and fuzzy, and much better, and Tammy-Lee's hair was dry.

There were families around the room, and some of the children were still asleep. It was quieter, except for a man with a woolly microphone that looked like a cat's tail. Followed by a cameraman, he was interviewing people very loudly.

'This disaster has brought the whole community together,' he was saying. 'And families made homeless by these terrible floods are still coming in...'

His voice made me drowsy, and I drifted off to sleep again, this time in TammyLee's arms. She was yawning and snoozing too, and Amber was stretched out on the floor, snoring. We were all exhausted.

'Wake up, Tallulah, quickly.' My angel whispered urgently to me. 'This is very important.'

Instantly, I was sitting up, on full alert, my whiskers twitching. Something was going to happen.

Chapter Fifteen

FROM A DISTANCE

'You are needed, now more than ever, Tallulah,' said my angel, and for once, she was crystal clear in her iridescent colours. She was so radiant that I thought one of us was going to die. I looked at Amber, and she was breathing. I looked at TammyLee and there was a strange light around her. Squinting my eyes, I watched until the face of a golden angel materialised from its blaze. I'd never seen her before.

'Who is she?' I asked.

'She is the mother love angel,' said my angel, respectfully.

I studied the new angel, fascinated by the swerving colours of her robe: intense pink, aqua and silver white. Mysterious images and pictures flickered in the energy she was generating, constantly changing. For one fleeting moment, I saw a cat's face, and it was my own mother, Jessica, and then she was gone, like something melting in the sun. She hadn't liked me when I was a kitten, but now her brief appearance had radiated love, which made me glow with happiness. I wanted to play and jump in the air, but I was restrained by the cat harness.

'Be calm,' said my angel, 'and do exactly what I tell you. Exactly. Now ... watch the door.'

As she spoke, a new family was coming in through the door, a young mum with a little boy who was dressed in a tiny denim jacket and jeans. Their pushchair was laden with bags of food and toys. Like most of the new arrivals, they seemed stressed and anxious, and stood looking round the hall for somewhere to sit.

'Meow, as loud as you can, and put your tail up,' said my angel urgently.

My voice called out, an echoing meow, and another, and another. Amber woke up with a jump, and so did TammyLee.

'What's the matter, Tallulah?'

'Keep meowing,' said my angel. 'You are calling that family.'

I did, and the little boy turned his head and looked at me with bright blue eyes.

'Tat!' he squealed, and tugged at his mother's arm. 'Look!'

I changed my voice to a purr-meow. The little boy was Rocky, and he was running towards me, and towards his true mother, TammyLee.

It was a mesmerising moment, and I sensed the angels forming a circle of light around us, weaving it into a celestial umbrella, sheltering us ... Amber and TammyLee, me and Rocky.

With sudden clarity, I understood the nature of miracles. The flood disaster had turned out to be a blessing for TammyLee.

'Don't strangle the poor cat!' Kaye came bustling after Rocky, a smile of humour in her eyes.

The reality of Rocky was exciting for me. He was bigger, and confident on his feet, square and sturdy as he stood gazing right into my soul with those unforgettable eyes. I could hear him breathing, and feel his vibrant energy.

He didn't look at TammyLee, but sat on the floor and put his face close to mine. I responded by kissing him on the nose, and purring. He squealed and laughed and wrapped his little arms around me.

'Tat mine,' he said, and I struggled out of his tight grip, being careful not to scratch him. He touched my tail and felt my whiskers, he put his ear against me and listened to my purr. 'Tat purr,' he said in delight, and tried to imitate the sound. I rolled over on my back, and he examined the pink pads of my paws.

'Gently ... gently,' said Kaye, breaking into our circle of light. She looked at TammyLee. 'I am sorry,' she said, 'but he does love cats ... and dogs,' she added, as Amber tried to get in on the act by squirming along the floor. 'Is your dog OK with children?'

'She loves them,' said TammyLee. She smiled at Rocky, but he still didn't look at her. He was only interested in me.

'We've just arrived,' Kaye said. 'D'you mind if we sit ourselves down next to you? Our house isn't actually flooded, but the water's rising and they've evacuated the whole street. I grabbed as much as I could. My husband's gone to work. I've got some chocolate and crisps, if you want some. Is your house flooded?'

They chatted about floods while I played with Rocky, and I heard TammyLee telling Kaye how she'd waded, alone, through the icy water to get home. How Amber had found her and guided her away from the riverbank.

'Sounds like she's a brave dog,' she said, fondling Amber, who was now leaning against her legs, looking up at her adoringly. 'And you're a bit of a heroine too. Did you say your mum is in hospital?'

'Yes, but she's OK,' TammyLee said. 'My mum is disabled, but she's a really special person. I love her to bits. I'm her carer, you see, and have been since I was ten.'

Kaye looked at her with wide eyes. 'That's AWESOME!'

TammyLee shrugged, but she looked pleased. 'So what about you, Kaye? What's your little boy's name?'

'Rocky.'

A shock rippled through TammyLee, but she acted normal.

'Go to her,' said my angel, and I stepped gracefully out of Rocky's arms and jumped on to TammyLee's lap. Rocky stood close, looking at her now that she'd got me cuddled against her heart. It was beating very fast.

'That's a nice name,' she said. 'Did you choose it for a reason?'

Kaye hesitated. 'I didn't choose it,' she said, and her eyes looked candidly at TammyLee. 'I started out as his foster mum but now we have legally adopted him, at last! His real mother...' she lowered her voice, '...aban-

249

doned him under a tree by the river.'

The circle of angel light tightened around us. If I hadn't been there, TammyLee might have panicked or run away. She kept stroking me. I was grounding her.

'That's awful,' she muttered, not looking at Kaye's bright open face. 'So ... how old is he?'

'Eighteen months, and he's great,' said Kaye. 'A bit of a handful, but a real boy, aren't you, Rocky?'

Rocky was standing close to TammyLee, playing with her bangles, and stretching up to smooth my fur with his tiny hand.

'Move up higher,' said my angel, and I manoeuvred myself up to TammyLee's shoulder, and draped myself around her neck, my tail hanging down one side and my face on the other. I had eye contact with Rocky and, after two purr-meows and a touch of sparkle, he looked solemnly at TammyLee, who couldn't take her eyes off him.

'Do you want to sit on my lap, Rocky?' she asked. 'Then you can stroke Tallulah. She loves you.'

'Loolah,' said Rocky, as if my name was a delicious chocolate. 'Loolah.'

TammyLee helped him onto her lap.

'He'll probably go to sleep,' said Kaye. 'He usually does about mid-morning.'

'I don't mind,' said TammyLee. She was acting cool, but hardly breathing as Rocky settled on her lap and lay back in the crook of her arm. They gazed and gazed into each other's eyes.

'This moment will last for ever,' said my angel, and all the angels in the golden circle were humming a lullaby, and winding streamers of stars around the three of us. The mother love angel flickered behind Tammy-Lee, bending over her with shining arms.

Rocky's eyes began to close, the dark lashes falling over his rounded cheeks as he went to sleep instantly. TammyLee rocked him and rested her face against his silky head.

Kaye took out her mobile phone. 'I've got to have a photo of that,' she said, 'it's so sweet, with the cat there.'

'Will you do one on my mobile too?' asked TammyLee. 'It's in my bag.'

'OK.'

'That's very, very...' TammyLee seemed stuck for words as Kaye showed us the photo she'd taken. '...Special,' she said finally. 'Look, Tallulah.' Inside her mobile was a tiny image of Rocky's sleeping face, and her face, and me like a fairy cat, and a bit of Amber's face too.

Only I knew how precious that photo would be. I filled the silence with purring. A question was burning in TammyLee's mind, and eventually, she managed to let it come out.

'What ... would happen, Kaye, if the real mother showed up?'

'She'd have no chance,' said Kaye. 'Not now that he's legally adopted. She wouldn't be allowed any contact. BUT ... she ought to own up really, for Rocky's sake. He'll know he's adopted, and maybe, when he's a man, he'll want to trace his birth mother. So, if she is out there, and she cares, she should come clean about it, and get her details put in his birth file, so that he can find her, if he wants to. And she should write him a beautiful letter to have when he's grown up. I hope she does, for Rocky's sake. I mean, maybe she was just a scared teenager ... they're not going to send her to prison, are they?'

TammyLee nodded slowly, and the silence sparkled around her as she held her sleeping child.

'She knows,' said my angel. 'She knows what she must do.'

I could feel the change in TammyLee. A calmness, a knowing, a sense of peace. A golden time of holding her secret child, sealed for ever by the angels.

'It was me,' said TammyLee, as four pairs of eyes stared intently at her.

We were protecting TammyLee, Amber leaning firmly against her legs, and me sitting on her lap, gazing into her soul. Fear danced in her green eyes, yet they shone with courage and maternal defensiveness. I was proud to be her cat.

The house was quiet now, after a long day of noise and energy from downstairs. The water had gone, leaving mud over everything, the sofa was out in the garden, and people who Max called volunteers had been sweeping and scrubbing all day. A new fire was roaring up the chimney, its blaze filling the sodden house with welcome heat.

Amber and I had a new bed each, and we were cosy in the spare room with the freedom to pad around the upstairs. I had a new cat-nip mouse and the walls reverberated with the sound of Amber gnawing a huge bone she'd been given.

The volunteers had just turned up, and the most surprising one was Dylan. He didn't say much but shrugged and grunted as he worked fiendishly beside TammyLee, tearing up wet carpets and washing mud from the walls. Even Max managed to be civil to him. 'It's good to see you're not afraid of hard work,' he said.

'I don't need your approval, Pop.' Dylan's eyes blazed with contempt. 'I am doing it for Diana, 'cause she treated me like a human being.' And he turned his back on Max and went on dragging a roll of wet carpet out of the door.

Upset by the activity, I kept going to the top of the stairs and meowing. TammyLee picked me up and cuddled me, and explained everything. 'We're making the house good again, Tallulah. A lorry will come and take away the muddy carpets and stuff. Then another lorry will bring us a brand-new sofa and carpets, and one day soon, you can go downstairs again and it will be lovely. So don't you worry, Tallulah.'

After that, I felt better. The sun streamed through the window onto TammyLee's bed, and I slept for hours, only waking up when I heard Iris's voice and sensed the weight of her struggling up the stairs.

'It's disgusting,' she moaned, 'they should've done that flood-prevention scheme years ago, not let it come to this. Disgusting, that's what I call it.'

I knew why Iris had come. I'd been there with TammyLee the night before, when she'd privately told Diana about Rocky. Diana's eyes had opened wide, and so had her arms. 'Sweetheart,' she'd whispered. 'My poor girl ... what were you THINKING?... You know I'd have stuck by you... Oh, darling girl.' She'd held TammyLee in her arms, with the angels watching. The whole story had come tumbling out while Diana stroked her hair and I lay with her, purring. And afterwards, TammyLee seemed lighter and softer. The dark secret had gone. I saw the angels lifting it away, turning it into stardust.

The meeting had been arranged and Diana insisted it should be 'done nicely', even persuading a tight-lipped Max to organise a tray with a tall pot of steaming coffee and a swirl of biscuits.

Dylan was the only one arrogantly munching biscuits through the meeting, which began with TammyLee saying those words: 'It was me.'

'I TOLD you!' said Iris triumphantly. 'I told you it were 'er. Didn't I say so? Written all over 'er face.'

'Shut up, Mum ... just hear her out,' Dylan insisted. 'MUM!' he put a mud-stained hand on her shoulder and made her look at his compelling eyes. 'Don't make it worse.'

TammyLee glanced at him with something resembling gratitude, then back to Diana, who was looking at her with loving eyes.

'I did have a baby,' she began, and again the story emerged, this time clearly, without tears. Only quiet strength glowed from her aura, and everyone listened, even Amber, who'd been trying not to growl at Dylan. She told them how I'd been there, and saved Rocky's life, and how she'd regretted what she'd done.

'I know it was stupid,' she concluded, 'and wicked, what I did. And I've found out the baby's been adopted, by a couple who couldn't have kids of their own, and they love him. So ... I don't think we should interfere, and Mum agrees with me.' She held up a letter. 'We're giving this to the adoption agency, for him to have when he's older, if he wants to find me.'

Iris opened her mouth, and shut it again. That's when I sensed that the angels were totally in charge of our meeting.

'The best we can do,' said Diana, 'is to love that little boy in our hearts, always, and from a distance.'

I am only a cat, but in that moment, I felt like a human, with human emotions, as we all sat quiet, letting the words settle like leaves falling through sunlight.

I kissed TammyLee's face, and put my velvet paws around her neck, but something didn't feel right to me. I'd done my best, but the result was not what I'd expected. I wanted to stay with TammyLee, and be her cat, but there was a pain inside me, an old pain from when Gretel had left me in the hot car.

This time it didn't go away.

Closing my eyes, I floated into sleep, and those words went with me. 'From a distance … from a distance.'

I sensed that my fur was shining like a halo, and somehow I had drifted far away across the universe. So far, far away, but I still heard TammyLee's cry of panic.

'She's stopped breathing! Tallulah … Tallulah … don't die on me, please … please.'

Chapter Sixteen

I HEARD THE ANGEL CALL MY NAME

The last memory of my time on earth was the feel of TammyLee's face, heavy on my fur, her breath warm, her tears trickling around my neck. Her words wrapping me in whispers. 'Magic puss cat ... please don't die ... I love you ... I love you SO much.'

I tried to respond, but the life had gone from my body and it wouldn't move at all, not even the tip of my fluffy tail. My vibrant little heart had stopped, and my lovely body with its silky fur had died so peacefully, there on TammyLee's lap. Her love was enfolding me in layer upon layer of colours, and inside it I felt safe enough to let go and float.

The humans gathered around me like a protective umbrella, and I heard fragments of what they were saying: 'We always knew it was going to happen... Tallulah was a rescue cat ... look what she went through.' Then I heard TammyLee's howl of grief. 'But why NOW? WHY?'

Surprisingly, it was tough old Iris who was hugging the crying girl as if she would never let go. And, even more amazing, Dylan was brushing the tears from his cheeks with the back of his hand.

Cocooned in TammyLee's love, I drifted through a brightening silence. I said goodbye to the silver-and-white cat who lay limply, her soft paws gently curled, her eyes closed, a smile lifting the corners of her mouth. She was dead, but I wasn't! I was a spirit cat again now, a shining cat with a beautiful name, Tallulah.

When pets die, they cross the rainbow bridge into a special land, where they wait for their loved ones to join them. Humans think this is a legend, but actually, it's true.

I didn't remember the crossing, but the angels told me that TammyLee's love had made it easy for me.

On the far side of the rainbow bridge is a sumptuous land of downy turf and velvet grasses alive with sparkles. There are trees with blue leaves, and flowers with heady perfume. Happiness and sadness are intertwined, and both are beautiful, both are welcoming. Together, they form landscapes with domes and cushions of colour. You can choose to be sad and rest inside a cave of lavender blue, where it is quiet and still. In there, you can safely grieve for your lost friends, and peer out at the great arch of the rainbow bridge, waiting and hoping for one of them to come over. Or, you can choose to be happy and roll around, purring with a bunch of other cats, or chase the sparkles as they zigzag through the trees in a land that is timeless, seasonless and very beautiful.

I still looked like me, like Tallulah, but my fur shimmered with light, and I weighed nothing. I could turn somersaults in the air! So there were wild times when I chose to be happy, and quiet times when I chose to be sad. I learned that even when you are healthy, comfortable and free, there is still, deep in your soul, a hunger and a longing for close contact with your earth friends.

I could have moved on, into the enticing realms of light where angels lived, and reclaimed my status as Queen of Cats, but I wanted to keep my name. I wanted to be Tallulah and wait by the rainbow bridge for the people I loved.

The best look-out place was on top of the tallest tree. Nestled among its turquoise leaves, I spent a lot of time up there, gazing right across the rainbow bridge. How long would it be until TammyLee came over? I ached to hear her voice.

'She won't come,' my angel explained gently. 'TammyLee is human and she must stay on earth for decades, until she is an old, old lady. Sometimes you can visit her for a few precious minutes.'

'How do I do that?' I asked.

'At certain times, the veil between earth and the spirit world is thin,' she said, 'then you can go through.'

'How will I know when that time is?'

'Your fur will tingle, and you will feel a longing. Watch the veils of light in the distant skies. Sometimes they shift and become transparent.'

The first time it happened, I sensed TammyLee was remembering me. The scent of her perfume made me purr, and purr until I saw the veil billowing and parting like curtains, and I did see my TammyLee. In an instant, I was close to her in my light body. She was doing a lady's hair, brushing it and twiddling it thoughtfully, and she was talking about me!

'I had a beautiful cat ... Tallulah. She was really special. She died years ago, her heart just stopped. It was weak from all she had been through. I still miss her.'

She went quiet and I purred loudly. I knew TammyLee heard me, and she turned sharply to look for me.

'She can't see you,' said my angel. 'You are too bright for human eyes. But she can sense you, and that comforts her.'

'I was always there for her when she cried for Rocky,' I said sadly. Sometimes I felt my work had not been done successfully, especially when the angel said, 'She still does cry for him.'

'So I didn't really complete my work, did I?' I asked.

'Wait,' said my angel. 'Time is different here in the spirit world. Already the earth years have rolled on since you've been here. TammyLee has a job now, and soon she will have her own home and two little girls to love. And Rocky is a big boy now. Many more years will pass, and in the meantime, you can choose to be happy, or sad.'

I chose to be happy, most of the time, and I accepted that TammyLee was going to be on earth for a long time. Yet still I had that ache in my heart. I figured Amber might come over and imagined running to meet her with my tail up. I dreamed of the games we would play, the joy as we raced around together, the bliss as we curled up to sleep. Amber and I had been real buddies, and she'd inspired me to play the way she did, with ridiculous energy and enthusiasm.

I watched lots of dogs come over the rainbow bridge, and none of them were remotely like Amber. No other dog had such a coat of bright gold, and a tail that wagged so fast and shone so silver.

On one occasion, I did see a dog the same colour, but she was old and droopy. Her tail hung down like a rope, her eyes were dull, as if she could hardly see, and even from a distance, I sensed the tiredness, the weight of her, and the pain.

It couldn't possibly be Amber.

Yet something compelled me to watch this pathetic old creature staring up at the rainbow bridge as if it was a mountain. She was moving, but only just, crawling, dragging herself up through the deep blue side of the rainbow.

No, it couldn't possibly be Amber. Or could it?

I sat up. My fur was tingling, and there was a longing in my heart. And why was I purring? Such a powerful purr, like never before, a purr that sent ripples right over the rainbow bridge.

The poor old lump of a dog was moving faster. Her eyes were brighter, her legs straighter, her coat more golden. It was as if she suddenly realised she was free, she was not in that old body any more.

The transformation happened smoothly as the dog reached the highest point of the rainbow bridge. Her fur glowed, her silver tail began to wave like a plume, her soft nose lifted and her face shone with joy. It WAS Amber! As she crossed the bridge, she became young again, a magnificent silky goddess of a dog.

I ran towards her with my tail streaming and sparks flying from my fur. We collided in a whirling, squirming, tail-wagging galaxy of pure joy. It went on and on, and when at last we flopped down and curled around each other, Amber looked puzzled.

'How did I get here?' she asked.

'You must have died,' I replied.

'I don't remember dying,' Amber said. 'TammyLee and Max took me to the vet ... and Diana came in her wheelchair. It was SO humiliating. I couldn't walk, I was so old, and it hurt all along my back. I couldn't even wag my tail, and THAT made me so sad. I was the saddest, most useless dog. The vet said I had to be put down, whatever that means. They let me lie on my blanket. Max just stood there, with his cheek twitching, but TammyLee and Diana cuddled me, and Diana said, "Thank you for being our dog," and then I woke up next to this rainbow. I saw some other dogs going over, and I knew I had to try ... and look at me.'

I listened, spellbound.

'You've come home, Amber,' I said, 'This is the spirit world ... don't you remember?'

'But I'll miss Diana.'

'You can wait for her, we both will, but time is different here,' I told her. 'Things don't take so long ... not years and years like they do on earth. And you've got me.'

Our time together passed in a haze of contentment. It didn't seem like years, but it was obvious from the glimpses I had of TammyLee that numerous earth years had passed. She had two little girls now, and her own home with a tiny square of garden. When I managed to look at her eyes, there was still that shadow in them, the shadow of Rocky. I began to wonder if I would have to go back, and start over, and be her cat again. Until, one day, my angel called my name.

The sudden blaze of her flight startled Amber and me as we lay dreaming and sleeping. I was in the middle of an impressive purring session, which stopped abruptly as I heard the angel call my name, It echoed across the universe.

'Tallulah! Talloo ... LAHHHH...'

The angel swept her cloak of stars around us like a blizzard of glitter.

'Come quickly,' she cried, 'quickly, Tallulah ... it's TammyLee. Come quickly.'

She scooped me up and whisked me through the landscape, and Amber came lolloping and wagging, her ears flying, her face radiant with excitement.

'You HAVE to see this, Tallulah!' The angel parted the veils of light at a thin place. We all gazed through into TammyLee's square of garden.

Her white front door was shut, and a man was walking towards it with long strides. I could see the back of his neck, and the tattered rucksack that hung from his wide shoulders.

'Watch ... just watch,' my angel whispered, and we fixed our eyes on the young man's straight back as he stood at the door. His hand hesitated as he lifted it to ring the doorbell, and I saw an arm covered in tattoos, and a bracelet of black and silver.

He rang the bell.

He waited, nervously, a piece of paper in

266

his hand.

The door opened and TammyLee stood there, her eyes startled.

'Excuse me calling on you like this,' said the young man in a deep husky voice that sounded both confident and scared. 'But ... I ... have reason to believe that you are my mother. My name is Rocky.' He held out the piece of paper. 'And this is the letter you wrote to me – you said you wanted me to know you – so here I am!'

TammyLee gasped and flung her hands over her mouth. She peered at Rocky and, in that moment, I watched the shadow leaving her eyes, the light flooding in until they sparkled with hope.

Rocky held out his hand to her. 'I'd so like to get to know you,' he said quietly, 'spend some time with you ... if ... if you'd like that. It would be cool.'

TammyLee could hardly speak. She gazed at her son's face, her eyes burning with questions, with one big question, that was like a fire she had to step through.

'It's OK,' Rocky said, sensing it. 'I understand about you abandoning me ... and I've forgiven you, long ago.'

'Oh, Rocky! Rocky ... thank you!' TammyLee opened her arms wide and they hugged. 'Every day of my life I've thought of you,' she said passionately. 'I never, ever stopped loving you... I dreamed that one day you would find me.'

The hug went on for ages, and the angels wound ribbons of light round and round the two of them. At last, Rocky straightened his arms and stood with his hands on her shoulders, a wide grin on his young face. He hesitated, then added what seemed to be two magic words. 'Hi, Mum!'

They laughed with joy, and I was so entranced that I found myself moving ever closer, until I was sitting on the garden path like an earth cat. TammyLee peeped over Rocky's shoulder, and stared at me.

'The CAT!' she cried. 'Did you bring her?'

'What cat?' Rocky turned to look, and for one eternal, exquisite moment, I kept perfectly still in my shining halo of light, my eyes glistening with love.

I suppose you could say that I 'vanished' then melted back into the light, like spirit visitors do. But not before I heard the whisper I'd so longed to hear again.

'Tallulah... I SAW you! Magic puss cat.'

268

Acknowledgements

Thank you to my two friends, Barbara Allen and Joan Thomas, who taught me so much about animal healing, to my writers group for their support, to my agent Judith Murdoch for her guidance, and, last but not least, my wonderful Twitter friends.

The publishers hope that this book has given you enjoyable reading. Large Print Books are especially designed to be as easy to see and hold as possible. If you wish a complete list of our books please ask at your local library or write directly to:

Magna Large Print Books
Magna House, Long Preston,
Skipton, North Yorkshire.
BD23 4ND

This Large Print Book, for people
who cannot read normal print,
is published under the auspices of

THE ULVERSCROFT FOUNDATION

... we hope you have enjoyed this book.
Please think for a moment about those
who have worse eyesight than you ...
and are unable to even read or enjoy
Large Print without great difficulty.

You can help them by sending a
donation, large or small, to:

**The Ulverscroft Foundation,
1, The Green, Bradgate Road,
Anstey, Leicestershire, LE7 7FU,
England.**
or request a copy of our brochure for
more details.

The Foundation will use all donations
to assist those people who are visually
impaired and need special attention
with medical research, diagnosis
and treatment.

Thank you very much for your help.